More Clarinet Secrets

100 Quick Tips
for the Advanced Clarinetist

Michele Gingras

THE SCARECROW PRESS, INC.
Lanham • Boulder • Plymouth, UK
2011

Published by Scarecrow Press, Inc.
A wholly owned subsidiary of The Rowman & Littlefield Publishing Group, Inc.
4501 Forbes Boulevard, Suite 200, Lanham, Maryland 20706
http://www.scarecrowpress.com

Estover Road, Plymouth PL6 7PY, United Kingdom

Contributing interviewed professionals: Dave Camwell, Will Cicola, John Cipolla, Diane Gingras, Cody Grabbe, Jonathan Gunn, Chris Jones, Doug Monroe, and Ed Palanker.

Illustrations by Erin Beckloff. Illustration in Quick Tip 2 by Cody Grabbe. Photos by Jeff Sabo. Photo in Quick Tip 45 by Kim Stroes.

Collaborating editor: Jim Ellis.

British Library Cataloguing in Publication Information Available

Library of Congress Cataloging-in-Publication Data
Gingras, Michele, 1960–
  More clarinet secrets : 100 quick tips for the advanced clarinetist /
Michele Gingras.
      p. cm.
  Includes bibliographical references and index.
  ISBN 978-0-8108-7794-8 (pbk. : alk. paper) — ISBN 978-0-8108-7795-5
(ebook)
  1. Clarinet—Instruction and study. I. Title.
  MT380.G56 2011
  788.6'2193—dc22   2010047156

Printed in the United States of America

To all my students and to
readers of my previous book, *Clarinet Secrets.*
Thank you for helping me move forward in the
unending quest for better clarinet playing.

Contents

Occasionally in our lives comes along a book that, by virtue of its insight, pertinence, and brevity, brings a whole new approach to the multifaceted challenge of learning the clarinet. Michele Gingras' enlightening publication, *More Clarinet Secrets: 100 Quick Tips for the Advanced Clarinetist*, is just such a book.

Building on her earlier groundbreaking work, *Clarinet Secrets*, Professor Gingras' new book offers up an entirely different list of topics ranging from equipment (reeds, mouthpieces, clarinets) to the psychological (memorization, stage fright) to the professional (website design, stage deportment). With cogent descriptions of issues and solutions, she brings her many years of teaching and performing to bear on these essential topics for advancing clarinetists.

Who knew that there were so many things to understand and to be able to do better? While roughly structured in a crescendo from the specific (Altissimo Register Response) to the general (Keep a Practice Journal), Gingras' book can be opened to any quick tip along the way, providing instant gratification and motivation when the practicing slog is getting you down.

We all know that progressing on the clarinet is a lifelong pursuit. Our rate of advancement is seldom a continuously upward movement; rather, it more often travels in fits and starts as we vary our practicing, receive motivating and informed teaching, and have the patience to work through our performance problems. Nuggets of transformational advice probably don't occur as frequently as we would like, and we are mostly powerless to increase their frequency. With *More Clarinet Secrets*, however, you can accelerate that learning curve by scooping up solutions to problems in lucid and digestible bites.

Gingras' upbeat and engaging writing is quick to offer a breadth of approaches and links to other authors; she is not a writer who is only interested in her own opinions. With an optimistic and philosophical tone, she also takes aim at the whole "clarinetist organism," serving up enlightened information about stretching, exercise, nutrition, and overall wellness—and why they are important to improving your clarinet playing.

Whether this book is placed on your bedside table or next to your practice chair, it will become your favorite and most-cherished clarinet resource. I know of no other single reference book that provides so much intelligent and hard-won insight. Michele Gingras is that rare teacher and performer who has not only excelled in a variety of performance genres, but has given much thought to what she does and how she can pass that on to others. I applaud her generosity and openness.

In reading this book you might feel a little bit like a secret agent—afraid that other folks could learn these "dark secrets of the tradecraft" before you do. Do you suppose it would be possible to run out and buy up all available copies so only you can take advantage of these fantastic insights? Probably not. So all you can do is integrate them quickly into your own playing—and hope that others are slow to do so!

Howard Klug
Professor of Clarinet
Jacobs School of Music
Indiana University, Bloomington

Preface

With my first book, *Clarinet Secrets: 52 Performance Strategies for the Advanced Clarinetist*, my goal was to share some pedagogical techniques that I had found to be most effective over twenty-five years of clarinet teaching. Little did I know that after a revised edition and four printings, it would not only still be going strong, but warrant encouragement from my publisher to share some new ideas. After conducting an online survey to assess the amount of interest in a second book and receiving a large number of supportive e-mails, a sequel was born.

More Clarinet Secrets: 100 Quick Tips for the Advanced Clarinetist is an attempt to reach a new generation of students and to share secrets of the trade that can increase their chances of entering and thriving in the music profession. Along with extensive development of clarinet skills, musicianship, repertoire, practice techniques, and performance experience, we must now arm our students with additional advice about interdisciplinary performance, secondary specialties, stage presence, performance anxiety, people skills, grant writing, technology, work ethic, marketability, organizational skills, job searching, physical health, and even financial planning.

It takes considerable patience, hard work, and perseverance to achieve mastery on a musical instrument. Proper guidance is paramount to success in music, and part of that guidance includes finding resources that will provide up-to-date strategies to reach your professional goals. *More Clarinet Secrets* is a collection of little gems of information aimed at doing just that.

Some of the topics covered in this book were also covered in my earlier book. To avoid repetition and to balance the amount of information for each subject as they appear in the two books, the topics addressed in greater detail in *Clarinet Secrets* are supplemented by relatively shorter chapters in *More Clarinet Secrets*, and the topics addressed in less detail in the first book have been augmented in this book.

My wish is for this collection of Quick Tips to read much like the way in which one would approach a box of delicious chocolates. Any Quick Tip can be read in or out of order and chosen depending on one's mood, preference, or need. The topics are many, and the choice is left to the reader to decide which one to "taste" first.

In addition, I wanted to vary and enrich my box of chocolates by inviting a select number of guest contributors to bring their own expertise to the table. I consider myself very fortunate to have had the generous and enthusiastic support of several esteemed members of the clarinet profession who provided their knowledge and experience and agreed to be part of the *Secrets* sequel.

Because *More Clarinet Secrets* is aimed at advanced clarinetists, it is assumed that the reader has already attained an intermediate or high level of competency on the clarinet and has studied privately with a trusted teacher for several years.

The first seven chapters discuss technique, tone and intonation, musicianship, reeds and equipment, repertoire, musicians' health, and the music profession, followed by a chapter containing extra tips on such topics as college auditions, website design, and marketability. Each chapter ends with a Quick Tips Bulletin Board, which includes a variety of last-minute tips that complement each topic. The final tip, Quick Tip 100, invites you to add your own ideas and share them with your friends, students, and colleagues.

This book includes several health-related suggestions for musicians. However, the ideas presented here are not offered as substitutes for expert medical advice. Before you make decisions concerning your health and prior to beginning any exercise, diet, or wellness regimen, consult a healthcare professional.

The pedagogical ideas gathered in this book are the result of more than twenty-five years of hands-on experience in the clarinet studio and are based on the techniques I believe to have been effective for the majority of my students. I hope that the ideas presented in this book will serve to complement the many other ideas published in the vast array of clarinet books available today. Much like a box of chocolates, pedagogy offers a variety of choices and points of view and it is up to the reader to make the selection. Enjoy!

I welcome feedback and comments:

Michele Gingras
Professor of Music
Miami University
Oxford, OH 45056
gingram@muohio.edu
michelegingras.com

Michele Gingras is an artist clinician for Rico International and Buffet Crampon USA.

Acknowledgments

The creation of *More Clarinet Secrets* was made possible thanks to the support of many people and institutions.

I thank my colleagues who agreed to share their expertise in various tips by providing detailed information on some of their specialties: Dave Camwell (jazz clarinet), Will Cicola (website posting), John Cipolla (woodwind doubling), Diane Gingras (practice philosophy), Jonathan Gunn (E♭ clarinet), Chris Jones (parental support), Doug Monroe (military bands), and Ed Palanker (bass clarinet).

I express special thanks to illustrator Erin Beckloff and photographer Jeff Sabo. I also convey my gratitude to my friends, colleagues, and students who wholeheartedly provided ideas, inspiration, and editorial advice: David Blumberg, Jennifer Capaldo, Kayla Cicola, Mike Curtis, Lisa Drake, Stephanie Gering, Laura Goetz, Dan Hamlin, Patrick Hanudel, David Kamran, Whitney Locke, Jeremy Long, Mallory McDonald, Heather MacPhail, Vickie Marshall, Natalie Nazar, Katey Parks, Brad Pipenger, Jon Pischl, Tadeusz Smith-Jamiolkowski, Kim Stroes, Harvey Thurmer, Emily Venneman, Simone Weber, and to each and every one of my students who shared their unique talents with me over the years. I convey special recognition to Stephanie Sisak for her encouragement and muse duties for hours on end. A most special thanks to Renée Camus for suggesting a sequel to my first book, as well as Scarecrow Press senior editor Stephen Ryan, senior acquisitions editor Bennett Lovett-Graff, assistant managing editor Jessica McCleary, and editorial assistant Christen Karniski.

I express heartfelt appreciation to Rico International and Buffet Crampon USA for their support in providing funding for illustrations and photos.

I saved my most important appreciation for Jim Ellis, director of the business program at Lamar State College in Orange, Texas. As a writer, I remain with no words to describe the depth of my gratitude to Professor Ellis who graciously offered to edit my manuscript before my preliminary submission to Scarecrow Press. By "editing," I mean working tirelessly until midnight several days a week to help turn my pages into crafted finished products to present to my publisher. I also give him credit for reversing my occasional writer's block, offering clever insight on explaining concepts, and doing so with unending enthusiasm.

Finally, I wish to thank Miami University for its continued support for over twenty-five years: The Office of Faculty Research, The School of Fine Arts, The Department of Music, Dr. Richard Green, Dr. Judith Delzell, Dean Jim Lentini, Barb Wright, and Karen Mohylsky.

CHAPTER 1

Technique

QUICK TIP 1: THE HAT TRICK FOR SCALES

The study of scales will solve a greater number of technical problems in a shorter amount of time than the study of any other technical exercise. —Andrés Segovia, Spanish classical guitarist

Scales are the building blocks of technique and they are present in virtually each and every musical phrase we play, whether they are ascending, descending, or in various patterns such as thirds or arpeggios. The most important scales to learn are all major scales: C, D, E, F, G, A, B, C♯ (or D♭), D♯ (or E♭), F♯ (or G♭), G♯ (or A♭), B♭, and all harmonic, melodic, and natural minor scales.

It is one thing to learn scales and read them out of a scale book, and it is another to actually memorize all the patterns. Clarinet scales can be quite challenging, especially because the range is so wide with almost four octaves to conquer, and because the register key produces an interval of a twelfth instead of an octave.

A fun way to facilitate learning and memorizing scales is to learn them in random order by following these six steps:

1. Cut small pieces of paper and write one scale name on each piece. Depending on which scales you are working on, include major scales and harmonic, melodic, and natural minor scales. For example, write "C major," "a minor harmonic," "f minor melodic," and so on.
2. Put all pieces of paper in a hat.
3. Pick a piece of paper at random and read the scale name. Before playing it, think it through, formulate the pattern in your mind, then play it.
4. If you play the scale with some errors, put the piece of paper back in the hat.
5. If you play the scale perfectly, remove the piece of paper from the hat.
6. Do this exercise until the hat is empty ☺.

QUICK TIP 2: ALTISSIMO CHROMATIC FINGERINGS

Clarinetists enjoy the luxury of being able to choose from different fingerings for each note, especially in the altissimo register. There are closed fingerings that yield a powerful tone, and there are open fingerings that can be valuable technical shortcuts. Tom Ridenour's *Altissimo Register* is an excellent book that contains a wide variety of altissimo fingering options. Ridenour describes contexts in which to use various fingerings and even includes blank fingering charts for users to fill out on their own.

I find that the fingering chart below offers a very simple way to play chromatically, from altissimo A to C. The pattern is easy to remember and results in effective response. Here is an easy way to memorize the fingerings:

1. Note that the altissimo A has no A♭/E♭ key.
2. Altissimo B♭ is like a C (third space on the staff) with a left little finger G♯ key.
3. Altissimo B is the previous B♭ fingering minus both ring fingers.
4. Altissimo C is the previous B fingering minus both middle fingers plus the throat A key to correct flatness.

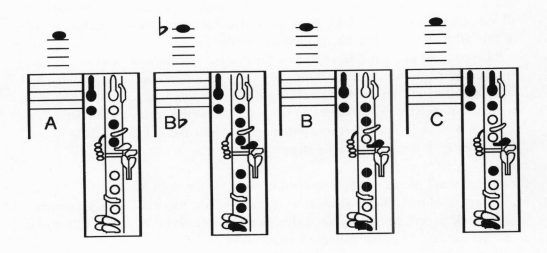

QUICK TIP 3: ALTISSIMO REGISTER RESPONSE

Advanced players who are ready to tackle the highest notes (altissimo register) on the clarinet may find it difficult to make the notes speak on a consistent basis. Oftentimes, the idea of playing altissimo translates into biting on the reed, choking off reed vibration that results in a thin and brittle sound or no sound at all.

Instead of biting the reed and pushing it flat against the mouthpiece rails, move your jaw forward (as if it were a desk drawer being opened) in small increments, depending on the note's pitch. Keep your top teeth in a fixed position near the mouthpiece tip, without sliding the mouthpiece further into the mouth while imagining a miniature set of stairs on the reed where each step corresponds to a specific pitch.

The following image illustrates the various jaw positions and their corresponding pitches. The higher the note, the more forward and downward the jaw lands on the reed. The "x" represents the point at which the teeth underneath the lower lip should apply pressure on each line.

QUICK TIP 4: HALF-HOLE THUMB

I have found two interesting ways to use the half-hole thumb technique. First, it can help execute a perfect half-step trill between throat B♭ and B or a whole-step trill between throat A and B. Second, it can help improve the response of the high register beginning with high D (third space above the staff).

A–B Trill

Play a B (third line on the staff), with the right little finger on the B key. While keeping this fingering, uncover the left thumb hole slightly, and press on the throat A key. Remain in this position and simply lift both index fingers alternately back and forth to create the trill.

B♭–A Trill

Play a B and while keeping this fingering, uncover the left thumb hole slightly, and press on the throat A and B♭ key. As with the A–B trill, remain in this position and lift both index fingers back and forth. The hidden advantage of practicing this exercise is that it will inevitably improve your left index finger technique by keeping the tip of the finger near the hole without reaching high on the A key. Your intervals will sound smoother and will be easier to play.

High Register Response

As shown in my previous book, *Clarinet Secrets*, the half-hole exercise with the left index finger is an efficient way to execute smooth wide intervals up to the high register. Instead of using the left index finger, try doing the half-hole with the thumb instead and see if it accomplishes a similar or better result. The left thumb half-hole is illustrated in the following photo.

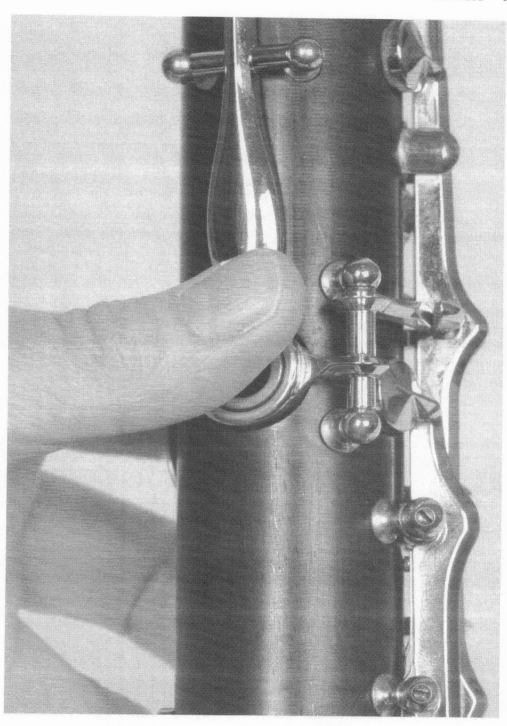

QUICK TIP 5: THE STICK ON A FENCE

Practice and hope, but never hope more than you practice. —Kalmen Opperman, distinguished clarinet pedagogue

Playing each and every note clearly and accurately in fast, technically difficult passages can be a real challenge for clarinetists and instrumentalists in general. A good analogy might be to compare this performance issue to that of reading a textbook more quickly than your brain can comprehend the words. The result can be that one misses important points. Playing technical passages at tempos beyond our capabilities results in loss of some of the meaning and effect of the music.

A similar comparison can be made with a stick being dragged across a picket fence (see the next illustration). If the stick moves slowly and consistently across the slats, the "trrrr" sound reveals that each "note" sounds clearly and evenly, making them sound fast and clean. If, on the other hand, the stick goes across the slats too fast, it skips over some boards, resulting in notes that will sound unclear and uneven.

When practicing scales and technical passages, work with a metronome, initially set at a slow tempo, making sure each single note is played at its full and correct value. Increase the tempo in very small increments, imagining the stick on the fence being dragged steadily and landing in between each board evenly. This takes patience and discipline, but the payoff is a crisp, clear, and mature technique.

Trrrr

QUICK TIP 6: HUG A TREE

Do you remember your childhood when you actually had time to do trouble-free things like hugging a tree? I have found that the feeling of a solid tree in our hands can create an awareness that we can use to develop lighter finger technique.

Putting your hands around a hefty tree illustrates that no matter how hard one tries to move the trunk, it will not budge. With this concept in mind, imagine that your clarinet has taken the place of the tree in your hands. Instead of hammering the keys during technically challenging runs, envision your clarinet as an immovable tree trunk. The objective is for your fingers to float gently over your instrument. An amusing analogy is to think of this exercise as playing "air clarinet" where your performance success relies on controlling your fingers lightly and with minimal effort rather than pressing on the keys forcefully.

In front of a mirror, apply this technique to difficult technical passages like the cadenza in Messager's *Solo de Concours* or the first movement of Mozart's clarinet concerto (bars 83, 110–11, and 148–49, illustrated on the following page), and see if you can keep your instrument perfectly still while you play. Once this concept is mastered, your finger dexterity will improve, and you will be glad you went down memory lane.

Bar 83

Bars 110-11

Bars 148-49

QUICK TIP 7: PRACTICING IN FRONT OF A MIRROR OR VIDEO CAMERA

Practicing in front of a mirror or a video camera is an excellent way to check on various technical aspects of your playing such as embouchure, finger position, body movement, and posture. It is also a good way to detect body tension during playing.

Mirror

Music stand mirrors are available at some music stores, or you can purchase a "locker" mirror with a magnet on the back and attach it to your music stand. Better yet, install a large mirror on your practice room wall.

To begin, play passages you have memorized so you can concentrate on playing without looking at your music. Some of the things to look for are finger height and evenness, flat chin embouchure, the amount of reed and mouthpiece in the mouth, the instrument's angle while playing, inadvertent raising of shoulders, foot tapping on the floor, and posture.

Naturally, everything you will see will be a mirror image so it can be a bit confusing at first. The good news is that focusing on your mirror image increases your self-awareness, which is a great way to prepare for a live performance because it takes you away from your zone of concentration, just as would occur in front of an audience. Moreover, using a mirror is practical, efficient, and inexpensive.

Verify what you have learned with your private teacher to see if you are interpreting your observations correctly. You may be surprised at what you discover while practicing this way.

Video Camera

Using a video camera or webcam is even better than using a mirror because you can replay video clips when you are finished playing and can assess each movement without any distractions from playing.

Position your camera or webcam-equipped computer on a table or piano surface to record your playing. Review the clips in slow motion to evaluate various techniques and save them in a QuickTime file to share with your teacher later on. If you are recording a rehearsal with an accompanist, save the good takes for your website or for future audition and portfolio materials.

These techniques are a great way to increase your rate of progression because you are being proactive and acting as your own teacher between lessons.

QUICK TIP 8: QUICK-ADVICE BULLETIN BOARD—TECHNIQUE

Never leave that till tomorrow which you can do today. — Benjamin Franklin, Founding Father of the United States

- Practice makes perfect. Imagine the serial number on the clarinet joint as being an odometer to remind you to keep adding hours to your "practice mileage."
- Although good finger position requires fingers to be relatively close to the keys and rings, all bets are off for trills. Lift your finger high when playing a trill to allow both notes to be equal in importance. Keeping the finger too close to the key or tone hole tends to make the lower note sound more important or longer than the upper note. Each note in a trill should sound equal in tone and in length.
- Do not collapse or "cave in" your fingers as you play. Check in the mirror for gently curved fingers.
- Trim your fingernails on your little fingers to prevent slipping on the right and left little-finger keys.
- Pick random spots in your piece to see if you can play any section out of context.
- Work like a slingshot: Take a few steps back and practice at slower tempos so you can propel your progress forward later on.
- Compare scales to street maps: If you know where you are going, you will make the correct turns in time. If not, you will get lost. Visualize and memorize the feel of an entire scale pattern before playing it to minimize risk of errors.
- Practice the chromatic scale starting and ending with E on the left as well as E on the right. This will create two different patterns, which are equal in importance.
- Always remember to play the high register C♯ (two lines above the staff) with no right little finger A♭/E♭ key, as this will avoid being sharp on the C♯. Use the A♭/E♭ key for all notes above the C♯ for correct intonation and ring in the tone.
- Mac users interested in a fun and quick reference guide for clarinet fingerings can download a very helpful chart widget. Created by Jeffrey Qua, it installs on the OS 10.4 (or later) Dashboard and can be found at apple.com/downloads/dashboard/music/clarinetfingeringchart.html.

- Use the metronome often and make sure to always keep spare batteries or use a power adapter to avoid interrupting your practice.
- If you miss a passage more than once, write useful notes in your music.
- For a complete regimen on how to perfect technique, consult the method book entitled *The Everyday Virtuoso*, by Robert Chesebro and Tod Kerstetter, published by Woodwindiana.

CHAPTER 2

Tone and Intonation

QUICK TIP 9: IMPROVING EMBOUCHURE ENDURANCE—EQUIPMENT

A strong embouchure is required to provide the stamina needed to perform major pieces without fatigue. Choosing the right equipment can help improve embouchure endurance in several ways:

Practice with Softer Reeds

Softer reeds might initially seem too easy to play and result in a thin and brittle sound. However, with practice you will notice that your air management becomes more efficient, resulting in a full and pure tone. You will use less air and energy to produce more sound because your air will be processed more efficiently through the reed. No air will escape through the bore without being processed by the reed first, and there will no longer be extra "air noise" in your tone. An analogy would be to compare a basic compact car with a high-performance car. A car built to reach a maximum speed of 100 mph will probably be overworked at 80 mph. However, if you drive a sports car designed to reach 150 mph, the ride at 80 mph will feel smooth and effortless.

Playing a softer reed will require adjustments on your part in terms of air pressure, air management, and embouchure control. At first, you may not like your tone. Avoid biting the reed and play with a tuner to ensure you are not getting sharp. Practice long tones, scales, pieces, orchestral or band excerpts, and your usual repertoire. Later, try gradually increasing reed strength if needed. With patience, your embouchure and airflow will adjust, and eventually you might wonder why you ever played on harder reeds.

Experiment with Various Mouthpiece and Reed Combinations

Your setup might be more resistant than necessary. Depending on personal physiology, a mouthpiece with a medium facing and a medium or medium-soft reed may work better than a long facing with a hard reed, or vice versa. The idea is to have a good, solid, full tone without having to strain to overcome excessive resistance. It is entirely possible to have a big and dark tone with a soft reed. Reeds that are too hard can result in a wonderfully full tone; however, soft dynamics may become airy and difficult to produce.

Teeth Cushion

Cover your lower teeth with a small, soft, and flexible protective pad, such as Ezo denture cushions. This can help improve embouchure endurance by providing protection for the lower lip. See Quick Tip 35: Ezo Teeth Cushion.

QUICK TIP 10: IMPROVING EMBOUCHURE ENDURANCE—PRACTICE STRATEGIES

Practice in Increments

Instead of playing until your embouchure gives out, try practicing for twenty minutes, then resting for twenty minutes, and repeat the sequence. The down time can be used productively with music theory or sight-singing exercises. After a few days, decrease your rest time by practicing twenty-five minutes and stopping for only ten minutes. Eventually, extend your practice to twenty-eight minutes, followed by two minutes of rest.

This process takes patience but, by extending your playing time in small increments, you will be able to monitor your progress and eventually your body will teach you what you need to do to improve endurance. The embouchure muscles will be "in training" just as you would train your other muscles for a marathon. To help keep track of your time increments, you can find an online countdown watch at online-stopwatch.com, or you can use the stopwatch feature on your cell phone, if available.

Oxygenating Embouchure Muscles

Musicians should follow the example set by top athletes by keeping their muscles supplied with plenty of oxygen. After playing for a long period of time, the lip and chin muscles build up tension and toxins, restricting local blood circulation and causing embouchure fatigue. Allowing blood circulation to return to normal will oxygenate the muscles and increase their performance and your endurance. It is important to take the reed away from the embouchure for a few seconds during rests to allow the constricted blood vessels to return to normal. Find additional passages to rest in your music, such as ones that are doubled by other instruments, and allow your muscles to recover for a few seconds during those opportunities.

Air leaking from the sides of your mouth can be an indication that you need a short break. Make a conscious effort to recuperate during rests in the music. Rather than simply counting empty bars, be sure to relax your embouchure and move the lip muscles gently to increase the blood flow. Muscles starved for oxygen become fatigued quickly, which can be painful. The extra oxygen will help to eliminate toxins and increase muscle productivity.

Rest

Rest and avoid stress before concerts, rehearsals, and private lessons. Since these events might last longer than planned and you may not get to rest when needed, plan your day so you will arrive refreshed and ready for the task.

Patience is key, so allow at least one month before deciding if these strategies help.

QUICK TIP 11: KNOT IN TONE

In order to play with a full and rich tone with relative ease, it is necessary to be able to produce the entire spectrum of tone dynamics beforehand. By practicing extreme dynamics, one can ultimately play regular dynamics with a full tone and without excessive effort.

The following illustration represents a long tone played in a crescendo, reaching the ideal "core" (knot in tone) and extending beyond that to an extreme dynamic level at which the tone would actually distort.

To practice this exercise, increase the volume of a long tone until distortion occurs (this takes a considerable amount of effort in terms of air support). Repeat this exercise and this time, stop the tone just before distortion occurs. Listen to the fullness of tone and try to achieve a full tone ("knot") with less effort than when you played the distorted tone. As you practice, your efficiency will improve and you will notice that it will take less and less effort to reach a full tone.

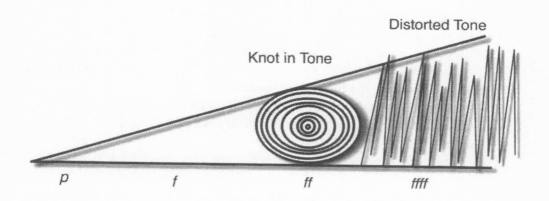

QUICK TIP 12: PLAYING WITH FIRE

Of all instruments the clarinet can best voice a note quietly, make it swell, decrease, and fade away. Hence its amazing ability to produce a distant sound, the echo of an echo, a sound like twilight. — Hector Berlioz, French composer; from his *Treatise on Instrumentation and Orchestration,* 1843

A common challenge when playing a note decrescendo is to decay completely without any air noise. As you decrease the dynamic and amount of air, you must *increase* the speed of the air. When you end a soft note, end it with the diaphragm instead of biting the reed with the jaw. If you slow down your air while decaying, the reed will stop vibrating, resulting in extra air noise. A good way to practice increasing air speed in a soft dynamic is to play with fire.

I am always pleased when I find out my students do not know how to operate a lighter (this means they do not smoke). Here is a productive way to use a lighter:

1. Hold the lighter in your hand and extend your arm as straight as possible.
2. Flick the lighter to light the flame.
3. With your arm extended, quickly blow out the flame.
4. With your arm still extended, blow at the flame but this time, focus your air in a thin line as you would a laser beam and push the flame lightly without blowing it out (see the following illustration).
5. Increase the speed of your air until you blow out the flame. You will notice it took more air speed to blow it out when your air was concentrated like a laser beam.
6. Emulate this feeling on the clarinet when you play decrescendo.

Practicing blowing out the flame with a concentrated airstream will improve your tone as you decrease the dynamic. Never let your sound become airy. Keep it full and resonant, especially in soft dynamics.

QUICK TIP 13: PLAYING WITH A VERY SOFT REED TO ELIMINATE BITING

Biting on the reed is a common problem with the clarinet embouchure. It may seem natural to bite on the reed; however, doing so results in a small tone and sharp intonation. A thin tone does not project well and contains very few harmonics, making it less rich and less resonant.

Well-known professionals such as synthetic reed maker, Guy Légère, and Indiana University Professor, James Campbell, suggest the technique of practicing with a very soft reed (#1.5 or #2 strength). The first time you try to play with the soft reed, you may inadvertently squeeze the reed shut and prevent it from producing a sound. This will be the first indication that, indeed, you have a tendency to bite.

After practicing with the soft reed for a few days, you will be able to play almost anything without choking it against the tip of the mouthpiece. Naturally, your tone will be far from ideal, sounding buzzy, reedy, thin, and unappealing. Luckily, there is a light at the end of the tunnel. You will learn to keep your jaw open, allowing the reed to vibrate freely. Also, your airflow will increase, adding substance to your tone and improving your intonation.

Practice with the soft reed in a private location and unveil your success once you have achieved an embouchure that produces a rich tone. Use a tuner to make sure you play consistently at A = 440 Hz and keep your airflow at a maximum. Since your jaw will now be more open, there will be more room for the air to flow, resulting in a bigger tone and more accurate pitch.

It is best to use the soft reed for only a few minutes each day, as it is a little unpleasant for the ears. It will be worth the effort and sooner rather than later, you will get used to your new embouchure and play with a more professional tone once you go back to your regular reeds.

QUICK TIP 14: STOPWATCH LONG TONES

Practicing long tones correctly and efficiently allows you to play longer musical phrases with fewer breaths. One way to maximize air management, airflow efficiency, and embouchure endurance is to practice long tones with a stopwatch. Choosing a digital stopwatch (as opposed to an analog or mechanical stopwatch) will simplify your timekeeping.

You can find an easy-to-use online stopwatch at online-stopwatch.com or by searching various stopwatch sites on Google. You can also use the stopwatch feature on your cell phone if available. The following exercise is not only helpful in improving your air management, it's also very fun.

First, test how long you can hold a medium-soft note and write down the timing. Once you measured your longest timing, perform the following exercise:

Do a long tone for ten seconds. Follow with another long tone, but this time, add one second, for a total of eleven seconds. Take a few slow deep breaths between each long tone and start again, continuing with twelve seconds, thirteen seconds, and so on. Make sure not to skip increments (even though you might feel ready to do so right away), and breathe from the bottom up for maximum air intake.

Each time you succeed in adding a one-second increment, write down the new timing to record your progress. A good goal to reach is about thirty-five seconds. Ambitious players may try for about forty-five seconds after a few days of practice.

You can use the boxes shown here to monitor your progress or create your own numbering system in a practice journal.

If you do the exercise with one-second increments, the gradual increase in tone length will be so minimal that your body will have a chance to adjust and inadvertently teach you air management in the process. Additionally, your embouchure strength will gradually improve.

Do long tones on all notes in each register and try to reach the longest time possible (without overdoing it or feeling uncomfortable), keeping in mind to use the proper breathing techniques described in my first book, *Clarinet Secrets*. The tone should be clean and even, without extra air noise. Use reeds that respond well in soft dynamics and that are not too hard.

Try to add at least fifteen to twenty seconds to the tone length you noted on your first day. Long tones' maximum duration can vary depending on individual abilities; however, a total of about thirty-five to forty seconds is a general example.

To increase lung capacity, sit with a straight back with one leg slightly lower than the other. Standing up is another option.

After two or three weeks, test your improvement by practicing long solos such as the slow movements from Rachmaninov's *Second Symphony* and Beethoven's *Seventh Symphony* or any slow movements from your solo, chamber, or ensemble repertoire. Practice slow excerpts or pieces over and over, and you will notice how the effort level will decrease over time, much like an athlete training for a marathon.

A good way to document your progress is to create a small journal dedicated to long tones. Write the date of each practice and the longest timing of each note you achieved that day.

Example:
Date:
C major scale:
Note:

	C	D	E	F	G	A	B	C
Timing:	10	10	10	10	10	10	10	10
	11	11	11	11	11	11	11	11
	12	12	12	12	12	12	12	12
	13	13	13	13	13	13	13	13
	14	14	14	14	14	14	14	14
	15	15	15	15	15	15	15	15
	etc.							

My longest time today is:

QUICK TIP 15: THREE-STEP EMBOUCHURE

In my previous book, *Clarinet Secrets*, I discuss the importance of a flat chin embouchure to achieve a centered and resonant tone.

Here, I would like to address how to maximize tone by practicing the three-step embouchure. Students often form their embouchures in two steps: take in the mouthpiece and seal the lips around it. Adding a third step of taking in more reed before forming a seal around the mouthpiece allows the reed to vibrate more freely, resulting in a bigger and darker tone. The three steps are:

1. Place the top teeth near the tip of the mouthpiece.
2. Without moving the top teeth down the mouthpiece, slide the lower lip and jaw down the reed to the point at which the reed meets the mouthpiece rail.
3. Bring the lips' corners inward in an "O" shape, flatten the chin, and blow.

Note that step number two is particularly important because taking in more reed prevents biting and sharpness. The result is a more resonant tone and more accurate intonation.

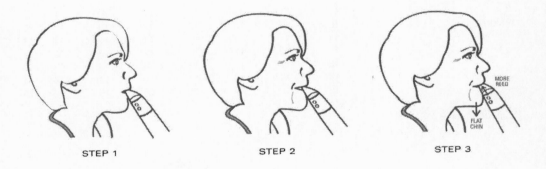

STEP 1   STEP 2   STEP 3

QUICK TIP 16: THE TONE IS RINGING!

For years, clarinetists can bite on the reed without noticing the effects it has on tone and intonation. This is because even with the biting a clarinet tone can sound clean, clear, and pleasant to less experienced players. However, once the ear matures and craves greater complexity of tone, perceptions can change drastically.

Playing with a silent tuner that displays pitch placement is useful; however, I believe that intonation is best corrected by the *ear* rather than by the *eye*. For this reason, I advocate practicing with a tuner drone sounding in the background. An effective approach is to play a scale against a continuous drone. While you change notes, correct and adjust each *interval* rather than simply correcting each individual note. Notice the distance between notes, much as string players do.

You may become aware that many notes in the clarion are quite sharp, such as D and D♯ (fourth line on staff) and G (top of the staff). Significant adjustments will have to be made with the jaw to correct these notes consistently. Lowering the jaw will help flatten the pitch and create more room for airflow. This embouchure shift may take a while to internalize, but with practice, when the ear anticipates a flatter pitch, the body will follow with the correct jaw position.

Harmonics and the Eardrum

Biting on the reed results in the upper harmonics being squeezed away, leaving the tone with a simple quality and sharp intonation. When playing a note with the jaw in a lower position and with more airflow, notice the pitch flattening and hear the added resonance and complexity in your tone. For example, play a C (two lines above the staff) with a squeezed embouchure followed by playing the C with an open jaw. Notice how the ear almost "rattles" or "rings" when the pitch is lower. The new harmonics created by an unrestricted embouchure and airflow add interesting complexity to the tone, resulting in a ringing of the eardrum. In short, if your ear is not ringing when you are playing in the clarion and high registers, harmonics are missing and chances are your intonation is sharp.

A visual exercise with color can be used to illustrate complexity of tone. Look at a white object and make yourself aware of how your eyes react to the simple and basic color. Then look at a bright, neon pink or lime green object. Notice how your eye is stimulated by the color complexity and how more noticeable the object is to the eye. The many colors contained in the neon make the eyes "work" harder, just as the ear processes more sound elements with a tone that contains harmonics.

Pay attention to your eardrums and how they react to tone. When the tone is ringing, the fun begins.

QUICK TIP 17: TONE TREE

A full and resonant clarinet tone has a core (or center), surrounded by an outer envelope of overtones. I like to compare a beautiful clarinet tone to the parts of a tree. The tree's cylindrical trunk, with water and nutrients flowing through it, represents the center of the clarinet tone. The protective bark represents the harmonics (or overtones) surrounding the tone's center, and figuratively holds the tone together. This illustrates how important it is to keep the tone centered with no excessive edge escaping through the "bark." This analogy helps one to recognize the adjustments necessary to create a warmer and more vibrant tone.

QUICK TIP 18: GROWLING

Growling is a technique that can add a wonderful effect to jazz, pop, and klezmer music. Singing a note into the clarinet while simultaneously playing creates the growl, and its intensity depends on the amount of dissonance created by the two different notes.

Learning to sing while playing can be tricky because players are used to blowing through the bore without vibrating the vocal cords. A helpful preliminary exercise is to whistle a note and sing a note at the same time. You can also practice singing while blowing air into the palm of your hand or through a drinking straw.

Although growling is most effective in the upper register, it is easiest to practice it in the lower register at first. Play a low note and simultaneously sing the note a fifth above. For example, if your voice range allows, play a low E while singing the B above it. If one or both notes do not come out, try singing the written B through the bore without playing. Then increase your singing volume and airflow until the clarinet low E comes out. Experiment with singing different notes against the note you are playing. Play a long tone while glissing up and down with your voice through the bore.

Once you have achieved initial success, it is important to balance the voice and the clarinet volumes. Record yourself to verify evenness and determine which notes produce the best growl.

One problem is that sometimes beginners tend to overuse the growling effect which may cause some throat irritation.

An excellent resource to practice singing while playing is Ronald L. Caravan's *Preliminary Exercises & Etudes in Contemporary Techniques for Clarinet*, published by Ethos. The book contains preliminary exercises such as *Matching Pitches*, *Scales with Pedal*, *Scales in Parallel Thirds*, *Scales in Thirds in Canonic Pattern*, *Intervals*, and *Melodic Leaps*. Caravan also composed a piece in 1976, entitled: *Five Duets for One Clarinetist*.

Other interesting applications with singing are:

1. Play parallel intervals.
2. Play melodic lines with accompaniment (alternate clarinet and voice lines as the melody).
3. Move the voice line against a nonmoving clarinet note, and vice versa.
4. Play a canon such as *Frère Jacques** with both your clarinet and your voice.

---

*See author's demonstration of growling and singing a canon on her Secret 47: Special Effects videocast, available on iTunes and InstantEncore.com.

QUICK TIP 19: TUNING GAMES

Once you become more advanced as an instrumentalist and develop your ability to recognize subtle variations in pitch, you can perfect your intonation skills by playing some tuning games.

Game 1: Playing Flatter Than A = 440 Hz

Play a memorized line while looking at the tuner needle to make sure you are in tune at A = 440 Hz, then calibrate your tuner one notch lower at A = 439 Hz and play the same line with the lower pitches. At first, this may be extremely difficult and your tone may suffer in quality; however, your ear will signal your jaw to open, which will eventually result in a more resonant tone and lower pitch. After playing with the tuner needle at A = 439 Hz successfully, test yourself again, this time using the drone. After a few days of repositioning your jaw to play at A = 439 Hz, do the same exercises one notch lower, with the calibration set at A = 438 Hz.

Ask a friend to practice the same exercises independently and after a few days, get together and practice a musical line in unison. Try to keep the line in tune together at both calibrations as consistently as possible. Play the line first at A = 439 Hz, and then try the same line in unison at A = 438 Hz.

Once you resume practicing on your own with the tuner at A = 440 Hz, you will notice how much easier it is to control your intonation and to play in tune, as well as how rich and resonant your tone has become.

Game 2: Intonation Competition

With the same friend, test your intonation ability by asking your practice partner to play a musical line purposefully out of tune and try to match the pitches as closely as possible. Ask your practice partner to play notes randomly out of tune (some flat, some sharp), as well as notes that are in tune. Bite on the reed to sharpen notes and lower the jaw to play flatter. After playing the line a few times, switch roles. Biting on the reed will only be done for this game and should be avoided in performance.

If you do not own a tuner, an inexpensive way to work with one is to use an online version available at seventhstring.com/tuner/tuner.html. Another helpful and fun way to practice with a tuner is to use the SmartMusic virtual accompaniment software, available through an online subscription. It visually shows how to adjust the pitch, and it can play a simultaneous reference note while tuning. The drone feature is helpful to learn how to tune intervals. Visit smartmusic.com. A microphone is necessary to make use of these tools.

The intonation competition game will undoubtedly result in some good laughs but is a challenging tuning exercise nonetheless.

Being proficient at intonation means that you can be flexible in all kinds of situations, including playing in tune with "out of tune" players. Your confidence as a performer will increase and you will be pleased to notice the improvement in your intonation control in advanced chamber and ensemble settings.

QUICK TIP 20: QUICK-ADVICE BULLETIN
BOARD—TONE AND INTONATION

- To keep intonation consistent, start with the tuning barrel pushed all the way in and wait until your instrument is warmed up before pulling it out. After playing a few minutes, the intonation will rise along with the instrument's bore temperature. Check with your tuner and pull out the barrel accordingly.
- Avoid puffing the cheeks when playing, as it reduces embouchure control.
- In order to play with the best tone possible, imagine you are dressing it up in a concert dress or tuxedo; always play as if you were performing and avoid playing with a "practice tone."
- Avoid air leaks at the sides of the mouth. Think of gluing the "wet" part of the inside of your lip corners together.
- Avoid biting on the reed. If necessary, practice with a double-lip embouchure for a few minutes every day, at least until you master a free-blowing embouchure.
- If playing feels strenuous on a consistent basis, consider changing to a less resistant setup (mouthpiece/reed combination) by trying softer reeds with more open mouthpiece facings.
- Avoid smothering your clarinet between your knees when you play sitting down. This hinders the tone of low notes and affects the intonation. Additionally, it may contribute to increased tension in the body.
- If you have a problem with a note (squeaking, cracking, intonation, or response), concentrate on perfecting the previous note, as the end of this note is the beginning of the next note.
- What part of the instrument should you pull when your instrument is sharp? In general, pull out the mouthpiece to flatten the left hand notes and the throat G, the barrel to flatten the left hand notes, pull out between the two middle joints to flatten the right hand notes, and the bell to flatten the low E and middle B.
- Avoid ending your notes with extra air noise. Keep the airflow moving to allow the reed to vibrate and the sound to remain resonant until the very end.
- When you end a note, do not end it by biting on the reed. Instead, keep your airflow steady and use the diaphragm to end the note.
- When playing soft dynamics, be sure to project your tone. Compare this to an actor whispering a secret on stage during a play, which is very different from whispering a secret on film where microphones amplify the sound or

in real life when a secret is told softly and directly into a person's ear. The actor facing a live audience would actually speak much louder so the people at the back of the hall can hear every syllable as well as the people in front of the hall. The same is true for a wind instrument. When playing softly, keep projecting the airflow speed, especially during decrescendos.

CHAPTER 3

Musicianship

QUICK TIP 21: BREATHING

Breathing is a critical element to sustain both life and musical phrasing. — Anonymous author

Music is arranged in phrases much in the same way that a story is formed in sentences. When we read a text out loud, we take the appropriate pauses and breathe where necessary. The same should be done with a musical phrase.

Oxygenation

Breathing is naturally important for sustaining a phrase; however, it is also crucial for maintaining proper blood oxygenation. Avoid sustaining a musical line for too long simply to test if you "can make it to the end." Instead, keep your blood oxygenated by breathing where the music allows it. This will not only help your mental concentration, but it will also keep your airflow constant throughout the piece. If you play until your lungs are empty, toxins will accumulate in the bloodstream so when you breathe again, it will be too late and you will feel out of breath even though your lungs will be full of new air. It will take a few seconds for blood oxygenation to recover adequately to allow the next note to be played comfortably.

Furthermore, if you breathe in while old air is still in your lungs, you will breathe in oxygen on top of carbon dioxide and, again, you will feel out of breath even if your lungs are full of air.

Planning Breath Marks

Breathing is part of the musical phrase and you need a plan that enhances the artistic result while keeping your body nourished with oxygen. Plan your breaths, write them in your music once you are certain of your musical decisions, and stick to your plan during the performance. In classical music, most phrases are formed in four bar multiples (e.g., 4, 8, 12, 16). Some phrases are nearly impossible to complete without taking a breath, so it should be taken at a logical place, such as at the end of measure 8 in a 16-bar phrase. This allows the phrases to be even rather than sounding lopsided.

Breathing technique is described in detail in *Secrets 32* and *33: The Body's Resonance Cage and Breathing* in this author's first book entitled *Clarinet Secrets.*

QUICK TIP 22: PRACTICE TACTICS

The only victories worth anything are those achieved through hard work and dedication. —Henry Ward Beecher, social reformer

The idea of "practice makes perfect" sounds logical in theory but can often be disregarded on a daily basis. Professionals know that seemingly endless hours of rigorous practice are the key to high-level success for aspiring clarinetists.

There are so many distractions, excuses, and reasons not to practice. Surfing the Internet, Facebook, texting, video games, and countless leisure activities compete for our attention. In his book, *The Outliers—The Story of Success*, author Malcolm Gladwell states that researchers have found that it takes about ten thousand hours for the brain to assimilate what it needs to know to achieve true mastery in a discipline. He describes the tedious groundwork stories of legends such as the Beatles, Bill Gates (Microsoft founder), Bobby Fischer (chess champion), and Bill Joy (math whiz). For clarinetists, success might mean reaching the level of proficiency required to seriously compete in auditions for professional positions.

Sergeant Diane Gingras, assistant-principal clarinetist with the Royal 22nd Regiment Military Band in Canada, former clarinetist with the Adelaide Symphony Orchestra in Australia, and my twin sister, offers the following practice tactics.

Tactic 1: How Much Practice Is Necessary?

Let's do the math. Our aspiring professional musician is a 15-year-old student who takes clarinet lessons and practices four hours a day. By the age of 21, this individual will have logged 7,200 hours of practice (subtract 60 days a year for the inevitable time away from practice). That is remarkable, but probably not sufficient to reach maximum potential. When you sit in an ensemble, you will invariably find people in the section who can tackle difficult passages more effectively than others. They are the ones who have mastered double tonguing or know the special fingerings that allow them to breeze through the music. Diligent practice enables you to master advanced skills that will make it possible to play virtually any part, and that is exactly the kind of musician a conductor or band director will hire.

Let's do the math again. Our would-be professional musician begins a serious practice regimen 1 year earlier, at 14 years old, takes lessons, attends music camps during 3 or 4 summers, majors in music in college, and practices 5 hours a day until the age of 21. This routine yields approximately 10,500 hours of practice time and performance experience, which should be sufficient preparation to compete effectively in the professional arena as a young adult.

Tactic 2: The Payoff

When you encounter an extremely fast staccato passage in band, such as *Italian in Algiers* by Rossini, do you have the skills necessary to play detached 16th notes at

132 or 138 on the metronome? To perform such a part, you will need to draw upon techniques and abilities beyond those of average players.

While attending a music camp one summer, authorities at the camp began searching for me after noticing that I had been missing for several hours. I was eventually spotted, emerging from a small practice hut in the woods. It was 8:00 p.m. and I had gone the extra mile, putting in an eight-hour day of practice. I vividly remember learning a great deal that day, as I did on all the other days when I put in my typical five hours of practice time, and gained a great amount of satisfaction from the mastery of challenging passages ever since.

Tactic 3: Making It to the Practice Room

One other tactic I use is a surprisingly simple technique that I developed in my younger years. When I lack motivation, I visualize my body going one direction, while my head remains right where it is. For example, if I am watching television, I physically move toward my practice area even if I am not mentally ready to do so. I take a few steps against my will with my mind still focused on my previous activity. I enter the practice room, open my clarinet case, and assemble my instrument, even while lacking the desire to practice at that moment. Once my clarinet is put together, I simply place a moist reed on the mouthpiece and begin to play. After a short while, my desire to practice materializes and I become engrossed in my music. The television program is long gone from my thoughts and the creativity begins to flow.

Tactic 4: Three Steps Ahead

You can do a few things to expedite your practice routine.

Step 1: Reeds

Make sure you have reeds that are ready to play at a moment's notice. Playing clarinet is challenging, so it is important to avoid struggling with new reeds at the beginning of each session. Set aside some time every other day to prepare your reeds so you can practice at any time without obstacles. This way, nearly half the battle is won, especially on days when you feel less motivated.

Step 2: Equipment

Naturally, you will be a step ahead if your equipment works well when it is time to practice. It is essential that you eventually find the best setup possible in terms of instrument, mouthpiece, reeds, and ligature.

Step 3: Practice Space

Lastly, keep your practice space clean and tidy so you can find everything you need such as sheet music, reeds, pencil, metronome, and tuner. The extra time wasted on searching for misplaced items can then be easily replaced by productive practice time.

Coda

As a professional clarinetist, I continue to practice every day to keep in shape. While some in the music world might disagree, I do not believe in putting the clarinet under the bed while on vacation. I chose to be a musician and believe that daily practice is part of my job. Dedication to one's career is essential, especially in professions that can be described as a "calling" such as in the arts, sciences, sports, and leadership positions.

I get satisfaction knowing I did the groundwork and went the extra mile during my youth to master my instrument. I believe in and live by this principle: "Work hard and things will come to you." The payoff is in the confidence that I can handle the difficult music that will inevitably come my way.

The time to prepare is now. The fulfillment begins tomorrow.

QUICK TIP 23: EAR TRAINING FOR CLARINETISTS

One problem faced by young clarinetists is pitch identification. Indeed, when a band director asks the group to tune to a B♭, clarinetists need to transpose the note in their mind in order to play the same pitch as the other instruments. In this case, clarinetists play a C fingering to match the B♭ concert pitch and internalize another note name, negatively affecting their note recognition skills.

Additionally, clarinetists face another interesting challenge. Since the clarinet is designed very well for fast technique, gifted players often become "technical wizards" in a relatively short period of time. Compared to violinists or horn players who must "hear" each pitch before playing it accurately, clarinetists can get away with simply executing correct fingerings to play technical passages reasonably well in tune. Although this offers many advantages, it can diminish clarinetists' ability to accurately hear pitch while playing.

Clarinetists who study ear training early on will immediately see an improvement in their technique because they can "hear" the notes before playing them. The combination of recognizing fingerings with the notes written on the page along with pitch recognition will decrease the amount of conscious thinking required, enabling the player to react more quickly. Additionally, clarinetists who are acutely aware of pitch can refine their intonation skills significantly.

Another bonus for clarinetists who study ear training is that they will be better prepared should they wish to major in music in college. Clarinetists who study ear training have better chances of improving their scores in ear training and sight-singing placement tests administered on the day of their audition.

Aside from taking ear-training classes in school or with a private tutor, some websites such as musictheory.net are extremely helpful in improving interval recognition. This website allows the user to hear and practice intervals by playing notes in succession or together with a virtual piano sound. Other training tools include theory exercises for notes, keys, triads, and chords. Theory lessons include music notation, note durations, measures and time signatures, rest duration, articulation, simple and compound meters, steps and accidentals, scales, key signatures, and more. The website is extremely easy to use and fun, and even includes a staff paper generator.

To be successful musicians, we need to make the most of our abilities. A well-trained ear is a valuable asset to help improve intonation and technique. The tools for ear training are more readily available than ever, and the sooner we get started, the sooner we will realize the benefits.

QUICK TIP 24: MEMORIZATION

Learning is easy. It's remembering that's hard.—Snoopy, *Peanuts* character

Memorizing your music is a great way to know it thoroughly and communicate it to your audience more convincingly. Whether you are memorizing a concerto for a competition or memorizing a marching band show, the benefits of playing without music are worth the extra time and effort in the practice room. On the other hand, performing a memorized piece with the music on the stand can reduce anxiety. Also, if the performer is not quite ready to perform without music, the experience can be distressing and can become an uneasy distraction for the audience. The following advice is intended for performers whose goal is to perform from memory.

Before memorizing a classical piece, make sure to learn it correctly first by using the music. Pay close attention to phrasing, tempos, fingerings, and articulation. In the case of popular, jazz, folk, or world music, it depends on the individual, but I suggest learning it by ear at first, and then tweaking details with the sheet music later (if available).

Memorizing a piece of music alone in a practice room is one thing; however, memorizing a piece along with the accompaniment is much better in the long run. If you practice the clarinet line by yourself, chances are that once the accompaniment is present, you will be out of your comfort zone and might be surprised at how little information remains in your memory, even after hours of work.

I suggest four strategies to memorize music with accompaniment as early as possible so you will not have to work on memorizing a substantial part of your music a second time.

1. Ask a generous and willing accompanist to work with you early on during your memorization process.
2. Work with the virtual accompaniment system, SmartMusic. Not only will the virtual piano accompaniment follow your tempo changes, but it can play the solo line along with you, play the piece at any tempo, and repeat difficult passages as many times as necessary.
3. When you are ready to play at the performance tempo, play along with a recording (or a play-along recording) while reading the music at first, and then without the music.
4. Once you have successfully played your entire memorized piece several times over the course of a few weeks, invite friends to listen to you. Having an audience is a good way to simulate the distractions that occur on the concert day.

It is important to plan how you will memorize your music in order to have enough time to learn the entire piece correctly before the concert date. If you do not begin the process soon enough, you may be pressed for time to learn the end of your piece and as a result, be less certain of those sections compared to the beginning sections.

Decide on a number of bars to be learned each day and increase the number by increments each day. For example, you may want to set the number at four or eight bars, depending on the length of the phrases, then add four or eight more bars the next day. As you gain experience, your memorization skills will improve and sections can be eventually memorized in a shorter period of time. Tips:

1. Before memorizing on your instrument, listen to the piece over and over until you know it by heart.
2. Sing your piece with and without accompaniment.
3. Make sure to also memorize all the rests and to internalize the accompaniment part by ear.
4. Practice your piece by singing it in your mind outside the practice room on a regular basis.
5. Practice the most difficult parts as daily technical exercises.
6. Work your tempo up gradually with a metronome.
7. Record your playing before and after you've assessed your progress and corrected problematic passages.
8. Intersperse memorization with other tasks on your practice list to test your ability to retain the memorized parts.
9. Visualize and notice note patterns as opposed to individual notes. Identify chords, scales, and intervals, and memorize left and right fingerings.

Example of a plan:

1. Memorize four bars on the first day. Analyze and understand the material theoretically, intellectually, and by ear. Continue your practice routine with your other material.
2. The next day, play the four bars you learned and add four more, for a total of eight bars. Again, analyze and understand the material and continue with your practice routine of your other material.
3. The day after, add yet another four bars, for a total of twelve bars. At first it may be tedious to memorize music but you will notice an increase in your efficiency as you gain experience with this aspect of your playing.
4. Be sure to arm yourself with a lot of patience, especially when learning very long pieces from the classical and romantic periods.

Memorizing music is challenging work, but the process will undoubtedly help you grow as a musician. When there is no sheet music between you and the audience, you will be able to convey your musical message more convincingly.

QUICK TIP 25: LISTENING TO OPERA ARIAS

A great way to expand your musical horizons as an instrumentalist is to listen to opera arias. An understanding of the singing voice can transform an instrumentalist into a lyricist and therefore drastically increase musical expression and tonal color.

Because the human voice is an integral part of the body with characteristics dictated by nature, biology, and physiology, the voice perfectly illustrates how musical phrases are naturally interpreted. Discerning instrumentalists can learn a great deal from the voice's natural beauty of expression by paying attention to minute details such as how great singers perform ascending and descending intervals, dynamic contrasts, and tonal colors. Similarly, instrumentalists who understand the operatic genre can shift from instrumental to vocal styles (and vice versa) within the same piece of music.

Four important elements of opera are the following:

1. Aria (song relating to the opera's story).
2. Recitative (spoken material between arias that helps move the story along).
3. Instrumental section (overture or instrumental section between scenes and at the end of the opera).
4. Vocalise (cadenza-like section sung on one or more vowels within an aria).

By observing subtle variations in dynamics and tonal color in ascending and descending passages within arias and vocalises, instrumentalists can more easily understand the natural flow of a phrase in instrumental cadenzas.

A great way to learn the many facets of opera is to see onstage productions either live or on video. Observing singers breathing with a correct posture and studying how their bodies move with the music adds another dimension to an instrumentalist's point of view.

A good understanding of these four elements can significantly improve the performance of operatic-style clarinet repertoire such as Weber's concertos, Rossini's *Introduction, Theme and Variations*, various opera fantasies by Verdi arranged by Bassi and Loverglio, and even etudes such as Cavallini's *30 Caprices*. By differentiating between technical (such as orchestral interludes) and lyrical (such as arias) sections, instrumentalists can add tremendous breadth and expression to their performance.

To begin, I suggest listening to a very well-known aria, "E Lucevan le Stelle" ("And the Stars Were Shining") from Puccini's opera *Tosca*. It is from the third act and is sung by Tosca's love (tenor) while he is languishing in his doomed fate as a prisoner. This aria is a perfect example because it is preceded by an exquisite clarinet solo with the same melody. My favorite version is sung by Salvatore Licitra on his CD entitled *The Debut*.

While listening to the tenor, notice the subtle gliding of the voice between ascending and descending intervals. Since the clarinet cannot precisely replicate this effect, subtle color changes in the tone can be used instead. For example, when playing a descending interval in a *ff*, end the first note with a sudden drop in dynamic (*ff* going to *pp*) immediately before playing the lower note. Think of the magical moment on top of a roller coaster where time stands still before the descent. This weightless sensation is exactly like the drop in dynamic of the voice gliding down from the top note to the low note.

Another voice trait that can be emulated is that of human emotion. While playing a crescendo, you might intensify the note not only by increasing the dynamic level, but also increasing its harmonic content. This can be accomplished by gradually adding harmonics to your sound as you crescendo (playing with increasingly dark and intense overtones with faster airflow), and conversely removing harmonics during decrescendos.

It is important to remember that even though instrumentalists do not use language or diction to express a musical phrase, they do use articulation. Just as the spoken voice enunciates words using vowels and consonants, instruments such as the clarinet imitate vowels and consonants by slurring or tonguing notes. Inaccurate articulation results in an inconsistent and unclear musical phrase. Pay close attention to all details in your music and adhere to the notated articulation as intended by the composer.

Additionally, it is fascinating to study details such as stage facial makeup worn by opera singers. The makeup emphasizes facial features, which is essential for the audience to notice accurate facial expressions from considerable distances. A similar approach is necessary so that words sung can be clearly understood by the audience. For this to be possible, singers (as well as actors) need to exaggerate enunciation and emotion in order to convey the intended message across the entire hall. Instrumentalists can apply the same principle and envision they are speaking and projecting a clear message through their instruments.

Listening to great opera arias can significantly transform your perception of phrasing and open up a whole new world of musical expression. You will be pleased to hear the subtleties in your tonal color and musical line once you develop and apply these concepts. Observing the singers' array of facial expressions paired with spectacular costumes and scenery completes the equation.

QUICK TIP 26: PLAYING WITH PIANO ACCOMPANIMENT

To create the best overall musical effect, it is important for the clarinetist to understand and complement the piano accompaniment. When playing a sonata with piano, for example, it is imperative to view the musical content as an equal duet as opposed to playing a solo with background accompaniment.

Some ideas to consider while playing with piano are:

1. Notice when the clarinet and piano exchange identical or similar musical phrases and make them dovetail into one another flawlessly instead of playing separate sections, glued together and disjointed. You might think of this as smoothly "passing the relay race stick" from one line to the other rather than taking turns at a passage.

2. When the clarinet ends a phrase with a long note, notice if the piano plays a moving line so you can complement the line instead of simply playing the long note for the correct amount of beats. For example, if the piano plays an ascending scale or a crescendo, try to mesh your long note with the piano line by imitating the dynamic direction and tonal contrasts, and by complementing the chord progressions.

3. Be sure to end long notes at the correct moment so they won't interfere with the piano's next phrase.

4. Practice with piano often so that your intonation will be as accurate as possible. Remember that a piano that is tuned correctly will play intervals without variation, while wind instruments' intonation can vary on each note depending on technique, embouchure, air support, and room temperature. Practicing with the online interactive accompaniment system SmartMusic is a handy way to prepare for rehearsals with piano.

5. It is important to choose a pianist who understands the art of playing within a duo (or chamber ensemble) rather than as a soloist. A chamber music piano sound and style differ significantly from a concerto soloist's approach. Both have merits, but an accompanist will know to complement the instrumentalist during various sections, depending on the prominence of the clarinet's part in the score at any given moment.

6. Although the clarinet and the piano have drastically different tones, it is essential to be able to match in tonal color when playing together. Listen to your favorite clarinet and piano recordings, and note how both parts mesh together.

7. The piano is a very rich-sounding instrument because of its huge resonance chamber (wood shell), so the sound continues to ring after the playing has

stopped. In contrast, the clarinet has a very small resonance chamber (cylindrical tube) and does not resonate after the air stops. To complement the piano's resonance, taper the ends of your notes with an almost inaudible decrescendo rather than abruptly stopping the sound.

QUICK TIP 27: QUICK-ADVICE BULLETIN BOARD—MUSICIANSHIP

- To keep tempo, tap your foot in your *soul*, not your *sole*.
- When you play tutti passages in orchestra, band, or large groups, every in-
  strument should exaggerate short articulations to result in the entire group
  sounding precise and clear.
- Listen to high-level professional clarinet recordings as much as possible to
  learn about and emulate phrasing, articulation, and tone.
- When you get near the date of a solo performance, practice with your concert
  clothes on and be prepared for this facet of the concert days in advance.
- Hear the pitch of notes in your mind before your fingers play them.
- Accelerando (as opposed to rushing) is good because it adheres to the math-
  ematical equation of acceleration (perfectly gradual), therefore it sounds more
  natural than rushing (randomly gradual).
- Practice playing very lyrically and musically without moving your body to
  see if you can execute expressive phrases with your mind without the help of
  extra movements. Once you have achieved this, incorporate appropriate and
  natural body motion to enhance your performance.
- Avoid being a "practicer." Although it is imperative to repeat passages to
  improve muscle memory, a player who plays sections over and over again
  can end up learning errors that are difficult to undo later on. Instead, play a
  passage and analyze its content so it becomes logical and easier to execute
  in the long run. Practicing intellectually instead of physically will help you
  remember the difficult runs more clearly the next day. I call this "thinkology."
- If you can get to the point of actually forgetting the clarinet while you play
  and only hear the music, you are on your way to mature musicianship.

CHAPTER 4

Reeds and Equipment

QUICK TIP 28: SELECTING A MOUTHPIECE

An inexpensive way to upgrade the performance of your clarinet is to invest in a professional-grade mouthpiece. Here are some selection pointers:

1. Avoid buying a mouthpiece just because a renowned artist plays one. Everyone's embouchure and abilities are different, so the same mouthpiece will not necessarily yield the same results for everyone.
2. A good mouthpiece will be easy to play, provide stability and consistency in pitch and tone in all registers, project well, have a "ring," articulate clearly, and resist chirps and squeaks.
3. If you plan on taking lessons with a new teacher, make sure the teacher agrees with your setup to avoid another switch once your lessons begin.
4. A long facing (surface against which the reed vibrates) requires less lung and diaphragm control and more lip control than a short facing. This setup typically works well with harder reeds and is often favored by orchestral players.
5. A short facing requires less lip control and more breath control. This setup usually works well with softer reeds and is often chosen by jazz players.
6. A medium facing usually works for most young players. It is easier to play in all registers and it works well with medium strength reeds. I usually recommend this option first, and then proceed with other options if needed.
7. When trying a new mouthpiece, check intonation in all registers with an electronic tuner.
8. Beware of "love at first sight" when trying mouthpieces. Play pieces from your repertoire rather than simply playing your warm-up runs. Reality will set in when you play repertoire rather than random (and favorite) notes. Play each mouthpiece for a reasonable amount of time and in various settings

(solo, ensemble) to see if the perceived air resistance increases significantly after several minutes of playing.

9. Try as many mouthpiece brands as possible. Once you find a model that works well, try two or three samples of the same model since there may be slight variations in manufacturing.

Mouthpieces can be found at leading music stores or online (some vendors offer special trial plans). You can also attend a music or clarinet conference where a large number of mouthpiece vendors gather in one place for a few days.

Once you have tried various facings for each brand, try them with different reed strengths. The idea is to find an ideal mouthpiece and reed combination. Choosing professional-quality reeds completes the equation.

QUICK TIP 29: MOUTHPIECE AND LIGATURE BRANDS

The most common materials used for clarinet mouthpieces are plastic (black or clear), hard rubber, glass, and crystal. Plastic mouthpieces tend to sound brighter than professional-level mouthpieces; however, they can yield excellent results for beginner and intermediate players and are very affordable:

1. Brad Behn Overture
2. Clark W. Fobes Debut
3. Gennusa Excellente Intermezzo (made by Ben Redwine)
4. Hite Premiere
5. Ted Johnson molded plastic
6. Leblanc Educator Series 2610 and 2540P Vito II
7. David McClune Plato
8. Pyne Polycrystal (clear plastic)
9. Rico LaVoz and Graftonite
10. Runyon (clear plastic, various colors)

Mouthpieces made with hard rubber, crystal, and glass are more stable and have a longer life span than plastic. Serious students usually opt for hard rubber mouthpieces sold off the shelf in the mid-price range such as:

1. Vandoren: 5RV, 5RV Lyre, B 40, B45, B45-dot, M13, M15, 5JB (for jazz). Note: The regular Vandoren mouthpieces such as the 5RV Lyre, and B40 are all tuned to A = 442 Hz. The 13-series mouthpieces such as the M13, M15 13, B40 13, and 5RV Lyre 13 are tuned to A = 440 Hz.
2. Leblanc: Larry Combs and Eddie Daniels
3. Gigliotti
4. Selmer C85 120 and other models
5. Pomarico (crystal)
6. Clark W. Fobes Nova
7. Portnoy

Advanced and professional clarinetists tend to invest in higher-priced mouthpieces that are made by artisans rather than mass-manufactured by large companies. Professionals often work closely with craftsmen who can make adjustments on the spot depending on the players' preferences. Various models are made by:

1. Clark W. Fobes
2. Michael Lomax

3. Richard Hawkins
4. James Pyne
5. Ben Redwine (Gennusa brand)
6. Greg Smith

Investing in a high-end ligature is also a great way to maximize the performance of your mouthpiece and reed. My favorite ligature is the Vandoren Optimum. Advantages of this ligature are:

- includes three different plates for various responses
- single, large screw allows for very quick reed change
- heavy weight facilitates very quick reed change as it easily slides into place
- sound response is excellent
- long life span
- relatively affordable
- comes with either metal or more affordable plastic cap
- attractive design

QUICK TIP 30: BORE OIL—TO OIL OR NOT TO OIL?

Various opinions exist regarding whether one should oil the clarinet bore. Some repair technicians also recommend oiling the inside of tone holes. I believe that it is a good idea to simply oil the inside of the bore as a measure to prevent cracking, especially when the instrument is new.

The two main effects of oiling the bore may seem contradictory. Oiling the bore prevents the wood from drying out. On the other hand, it creates a barrier that prevents extra moisture such as water and saliva from penetrating the wood. The primary benefit of oiling the bore is that it helps stabilize the moisture content of the wood, which can prevent cracking. Additionally, it helps prevent water buildup in tone holes by facilitating the movement of water down the bore. Lastly, it can prevent the instrument's tenon joints from shrinking and becoming loose.

I suggest oiling the bore of a new clarinet a total of three or four times in the first year as follows:

1. immediately upon purchasing a new instrument
2. once after one week
3. once or twice after three and five weeks

I believe it is not necessary to oil the bore after the first year. Note that some manufacturers advise against oiling the bore and doing so may void the warranty. I do not recommend oiling the outside body surface unless it is to refurbish a very old and neglected instrument.

Choosing whether to oil the clarinet bore is a personal decision. If done correctly, it can be an effective way to prevent the wood from cracking. Needless to say, never oil the mouthpiece and avoid playing on a freshly oiled instrument.

QUICK TIP 31: BORE OIL—HOW-TO GUIDE

To begin, you will need bore oil (see C in the following illustration), a brush, some aluminum foil cut in squares (D), and paper towels. Brushes made specifically for oiling the bore (B) can be found online, or you can use a "pad saver" (A). If you wish to oil the inside of the tone holes, you will also need cotton swabs (this extra step requires removal of the keys). Use only bore oil that is specifically designed for woodwind instruments. Very economical brands of bore oils are available at most music stores or online. Bore oil should never be used to oil the keys (key oil is also available at music stores).

Apply a very small quantity of oil by dribbling a thin dotted line onto the brush, spreading it evenly. One way to estimate the correct amount of oil is by testing the oiled brush on the barrel or bell, as there are no keys, pads, or holes. Insert the brush into the barrel and rotate it slowly back and forth. If oil drops appear, dab off excess oil with a paper towel.

Before you oil the upper and lower joints, protect the pads by applying small aluminum foil squares over each hole that is covered by a closed pad (E). Oil the lower joint by carefully inserting the brush from the bell end and avoid applying too much pressure so the oil won't drip from the brush. Be sure to evenly cover the entire bore surface.

Since the upper joint is partially blocked by a register hole chimney a few inches from the top, it is oiled in two steps—from the bottom and then from the top.

After oiling the entire bore, leave the clarinet case open overnight to allow aeration. The next day, clean your instrument with a silk swab and check for any excess oil where the joints fit together and on pads and keys. Lastly, remove the aluminum squares. The instrument is now ready to be played.

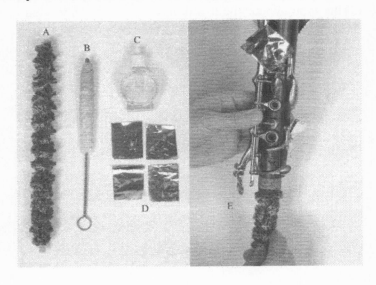

QUICK TIP 32: BREAKING IN A NEW CLARINET

It is important to carefully break in a new wood clarinet to diminish the risk of cracking (this also applies to an older instrument that has been stored for a long period of time). Wood is an organic material and will respond to various temperatures and humidity by swelling or shrinking. Breaking in your clarinet slowly will help the wood adapt gradually to climate changes.

To avoid excessive moisture absorption by the wood, refrain from playing your new instrument for prolonged sessions at first. This will reduce swelling and the potential for cracking. It is also important to prevent the instrument from becoming too dry. In very dry climates, some players keep a few fresh orange peels inside the case (away from the keys) to maintain consistent but low-level moisture. This is preferable to commercial products that can leak water in the case.

Before breaking in your clarinet, I suggest coating the bore of your instrument with bore oil (see Quick Tip 31: Bore Oil: How-to Guide). Although opinions differ considerably, my preference is to seal the wood with the oil before playing (only use bore oil specifically designed for woodwind instruments). This will not necessarily prevent cracking, but it will limit quick swelling (excess moisture) or shrinkage (excess dryness).

Steps to break in your clarinet:

1. Let your instrument adjust to the room's temperature before playing. If the room is cold, warm the top joint under your arm instead of blowing warm air through the bore.
2. During the first week, play the instrument fifteen minutes a day and swab it thoroughly after each session.
3. During the second week, increase your playing time to two separate sessions of fifteen minutes a day. If you cannot play twice a day, increase the playing time by five minutes daily.
4. During the third week and beyond, increase the duration of your sessions each day.

Never leave your clarinet in a car during any season. Heat and cold could do serious damage, not to mention that leaving your instrument unattended increases the risk of theft. Avoid storing your instrument in cold lockers or near heat sources. If your instrument will be unused for some time, leave your case open to prevent mold growth.

Repairing a cracked clarinet can be costly, so it is best to take all precautions to reduce the risk. If cracking does occur, take your instrument to a trusted repair technician as soon as possible. Cracks can be pinned seamlessly and effectively.

QUICK TIP 33: CLARIPATCH

At times players encounter situations with reeds in which age, environmental conditions, or other factors can contribute to reeds warping and lacking responsiveness. I have found that when reed adjustments fail, a Swiss product called Claripatch (see photo below) can help alleviate the problem. Claripatch is a thin and reusable aluminum-coated plastic patch (B) placed between the reed and the mouthpiece (D), designed to either fit the gap created by warping or temporarily modify mouthpiece's facing.

There are eight different shapes and thicknesses available, and the life span of patches depends on frequency of usage. The product is designed to modify a reed's strength (softer or harder) by altering the interface between the reed and the mouthpiece, enabling the modification of the mouthpiece's curvature without changing the mouthpiece. The patches can help improve the response of a warped reed by bridging the gap between the reed and the mouthpiece. I like to use this product in extreme cases where reeds simply won't respond adequately. At times, I found that the product adds a slight buzz to a tone when I pick the wrong patch size and shape. The various shapes are rated on a chart, and each patch is marked with the appropriate letter to identify sizes.

The professional version of this product is quite expensive; however, there is also a Junior set available at a lower price that contains fewer patches. Each set comes with a ring to hold the patches in place (C), printed instructions, and a carrying case. The professional package also includes a handy little practice mute as a bonus (A). More information can be found at claripatch.com.

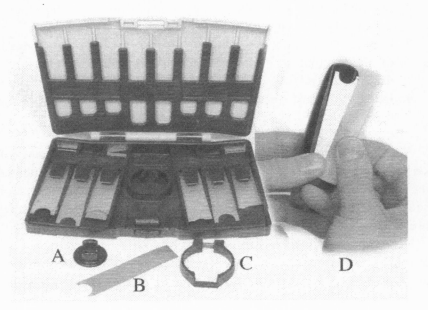

QUICK TIP 34: EMERGENCY EQUIPMENT

Sooner or later, it happens to all of us. You arrive at a performance, well-prepared and on time. You take your seat on the stage to warm up, open your case, and discover that an important piece of equipment such as your mouthpiece or barrel is missing. We have all left our music or critical gear at home or in the practice room, resulting in panic and risk to our reputations as dependable musicians.

I recommend that clarinetists keep numerous items in an emergency kit in their car and/or locker to help deal with unforeseen situations that can inevitably arise at the most inopportune moments. Examples are listed below and can vary depending on individual needs.

- Spare mouthpiece and barrel: Since extreme temperatures will cause damage, you should not leave your best mouthpiece and barrel in your car. However, keeping inexpensive replacements in your car can be a lifesaver.
- Extra reeds: As with mouthpieces and barrels, extreme temperatures could damage reeds, so avoid keeping your favorite reeds in the car. As an extra precaution, synthetic reeds such as the excellent reeds made by Guy Légère can be added to the mix. These reeds are also particularly effective with auxiliary instruments like E♭ piccolo clarinet and bass clarinet.
- Spare ligature: If for some reason you do not have a ligature or your spare ligature breaks, adhesive tapes of any kind can be put around the mouthpiece and reed at the last minute.
- Small screwdriver set: Screws and keys can fall off or need to be loosened due to weather changes.
- Lighter: This can be used to heat the glue for resetting pads.
- Rubber bands of various sizes: These can be used to temporarily repair weak or broken springs.
- A music stand light (with extra batteries): This is very useful when the performance space is not well lit or if you play a late afternoon outdoor event that continues as natural light fades. Always remember to angle the light away from the audience's eye level.
- Folding music stand: This is also useful to help out colleagues who are missing a music stand at the last minute.
- Clothespins: Snack bag clips or clothespins hold music in place at windy outdoor concerts.
- Sunglasses for outdoor concerts: If you play a late afternoon concert facing west on a sunny day, the sun will set right in your eyes.
- Earplugs: Brass instruments can sometimes sit close behind the clarinet section potentially damaging your hearing in loud, tutti passages.

- Money: Always have extra cash as well as a credit card hidden in your car or locker in case of emergency.

Everyday necessities such as repair material and tools, reeds, extra pad set, mouthpiece patches and thumb rest cushions, swab, reed rush, reed clipper, mini water container for reeds, folding scissors, adhesive tapes of all kinds, pencil, tuner, metronome, business cards, sewing kit, medicine container, contact lenses and eye drops, and toothbrush and toothpaste should always be readily available in the clarinet case or attached pouch. These are discussed in detail in Secret 42: Equipment Pouch in my first book, *Clarinet Secrets*.

QUICK TIP 35: EZO TEETH CUSHION

Irritation inside the lower lip can occur after playing for an extended period of time. Once you have developed a consistent embouchure with minimal biting on the reed, a protective, flexible cushion can be placed over the lower teeth to minimize discomfort. This helps improve embouchure endurance by providing protection of the lower lip and it makes playing much easier in the high register. However, if this aid is utilized prematurely, it can encourage biting, which is undesirable for a good embouchure and full tone.

In the past, single-reed players were known to use materials such as cigarette paper or dental wax sheets to protect the lower lip. Needless to say, cigarette paper is most likely made of carcinogenic material, so its use is highly inadvisable. Wax sheets used by dentists are available for musicians under the name of Lip-Ease Teeth Cushions; unfortunately, this product tends to be hard to find and expensive.

A terrific solution is to use Ezo Denture Cushions, which are nontoxic and easily found at pharmacies, grocery stores, and online stores. Cut the cushions to size and fit over the lower teeth to help make extended practice sessions more comfortable.

The following photo illustrates the various cutting steps from the original shape (A). First, cut a one-inch piece (B). Trim the edges for comfort (C). Fold the piece in half and place the cushion over the lower teeth and press into place with the tongue and fingers. Ezo is made with wax and therefore body heat facilitates

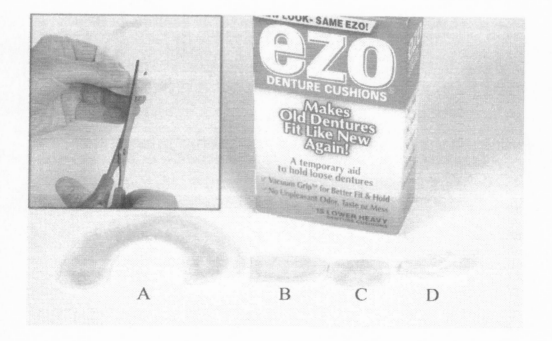

A   B   C   D

molding after a minute or two in the mouth (D). Cushion size can be customized to your preference. The material may be placed over braces and orthodontic appliances and can help with uneven teeth and smooth out sharp teeth that cut the inside lower lip. Once the material softens in the mouth, it is hardly noticeable while playing.

Because the strip quickly dries once out of the mouth, carefully remove it from your teeth so that the shape will remain intact and store the dry piece in a small box to protect it. If stored properly, a single piece can last for at least two weeks of playing.

A word of caution is necessary: Be careful when inhaling while using the cushion as it may dislodge and become a choking hazard. If molded properly on the teeth, it should remain in place, but safety should be the highest priority at all times.

QUICK TIP 36: MOLESKIN PADDING

It is surprising how many unlikely materials and products clarinetists can use for repairs and improvement on their instruments (see photos below). One of these products is Dr. Scholl's Moleskin Padding. This material is a dense padding, backed with a strong adhesive. Dr. Scholl's Molefoam Padding (A) is thick, and Walgreen's (or CVS's) Super Moleskin Plus (B) foot padding is thinner.

Here are three ways to use the material:

1. Keep reeds moist inside the mouthpiece cap and reed case.
2. Lower the pitch of clarion B.
3. Use instead of key cork.

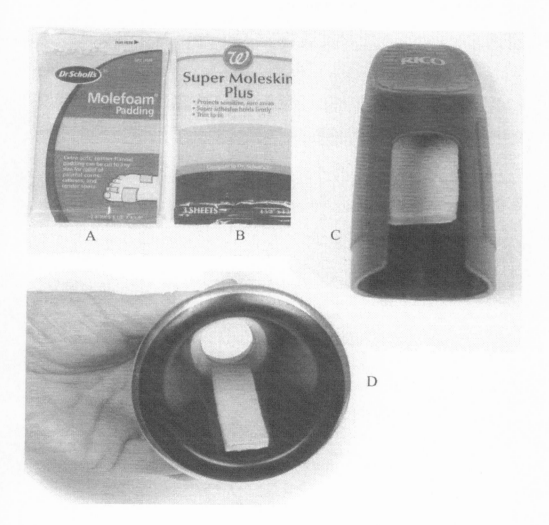

Keeping the reed moist when practicing, playing, or teaching over the course of several hours is a great way to ensure your reed's response stays consistent throughout the day. As shown in the photo (C), trim a rectangular piece and place in the mouthpiece cap facing the reed to keep it damp. The adhesive is very effective but it can also be easily removed when it is time to replace it with a fresh new piece, which lasts about a month. To moisten the pad, dip the cap in a glass of water and shake off the excess, or simply pat some water on the pad with your fingers. To avoid rust, use a plastic cap.

When your clarion B (third line on staff) is consistently sharp, place a rectangle of padding in the bell as illustrated in the photo (D). Be careful not to trim a too large piece so that your low E does not become flat.

Lastly, use very small squares as a quick replacement for key corks. Additional uses are limited only by your imagination.

QUICK TIP 37: SWAB REMOVAL TOOL

Because there is a metal register tube (or chimney) protruding inside the top section of the upper joint, it is important to be careful when pulling a cotton or silk swab through the bore of a clarinet. Insert the weighted pull slowly and make sure the swab is completely untangled before sliding it through the bore, verifying that the swab is not ripped or damaged beforehand. Silk swabs are thinner and slide more easily than cotton, so they are highly recommended.

If for some reason your swab does get stuck in the bore, I suggest freeing it using a homemade tool with a harpoon-shaped tip.

How to Make a Swab Removal Tool

Purchase a thin, ten-inch-long, flathead screwdriver and ask a key maker at the hardware store to grind the tip in the shape of a mini-harpoon, as shown in the photo below. For best results, use a pencil on the screwdriver blade to outline the hook shape to be created.

Removing the Swab

Insert the tool through the bottom of the upper joint as illustrated in the photo below. Twist the harpoon tip into the swab until it is hooked securely, and gently pull out the swab through the bottom part of the joint. Never try to pull the swab back through the top part of the joint and be careful not to scratch the wood during the process.

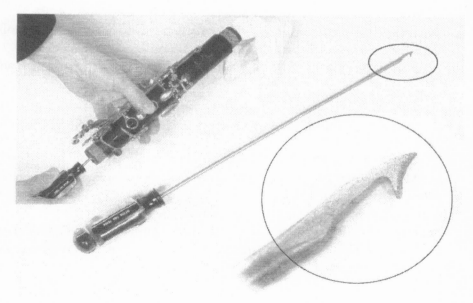

QUICK TIP 38: CLARINET MAINTENANCE AND REPAIR

Clarinets have complicated and sensitive mechanisms that require expert care. It is important to choose a store that provides superior service after the sale.

Daily care and annual professional maintenance will keep your clarinet in top playing condition, help it to last longer, and protect your investment.

Steps for instrument care:

1. Use cork grease regularly to lengthen the joints' cork life. Do not use it too often, as it can loosen the joints to the point of slippage.
2. Assemble and disassemble the instrument carefully by holding the joints firmly without bending the keys. Press down the top joint rings and hold the bottom joint near the bell without pressing down any rings so that the cork beneath the bridge key is not damaged by the bridge lever between joints.
3. Brush or use mouthwash before playing to prevent sugar or food particles from getting into the bore or on the pads.
4. Warm up the top joint under your arm if playing in a cold room. Avoid blowing warm air into a cold bore, as it may increase chances of cracking.
5. Swab your instrument thoroughly after each playing session. Remember to also dry the inner edges of the barrel, lower joint, and bell. Carefully untangle the swab beforehand to prevent it from getting caught on the register chimney. A silk swab is thin and flexible and absorbs very well. Some swabs have a clever pull-through design on both ends to avoid bunching.
6. Polish the keys with a clean soft cloth to remove excess moisture and oil from the fingers. Never use any products to polish the wood.
7. Occasionally remove dust and grime between the keys and over the tone holes with a small, soft paintbrush.
8. Take your instrument to a professional shop for yearly maintenance and bring a typed list of specific problems to be addressed. Ask the technician to replace pads that are becoming discolored. Better yet, have an expert upgrade the top joint pads with synthetic or cork pads. Although this is more costly, the pads will last much longer and are worth the investment. Have the technician repair broken key corks, tighten loose keys, and oil the keys, in addition to performing a general adjustment. Also have the dust cleaned out of the register tube.
9. Consider learning basic instrument repair.
10. Acquire Heather Karlsson's book entitled: *Care and Feeding of Your Clarinet: A User's Guide to Basic Maintenance.* It is very informative, easy to read, and entertaining.

QUICK TIP 39: MOUTHPIECE PATCH

There are two schools of thought regarding whether or not to use a mouthpiece patch. One point of view recommends the use of a patch to reduce the amount of vibration against the upper teeth, to improve the grip on the mouthpiece with the teeth for increased embouchure stability, and to protect the mouthpiece surface from sharp teeth (see illustration 1). The flip side discourages use of a mouthpiece patch because it might inadvertently tame down the mouthpiece vibration, inhibiting response in general.

I believe that the decision depends upon physical characteristics and preferences. A patch will add about 0.5 mm in overall thickness to the mouthpiece, forcing the jaw into a slightly more open position. This could affect tongue control and increase tension, as the teeth are held farther apart. A good demonstration of this effect is to compare fast tonguing with a "dee" and "dah" syllable while speaking instead of tonguing on the tip of the mouthpiece. Invariably, the staccato speed will increase with the "dee" syllable because there is less jaw movement and tongue tension while the mouth is closed compared to when it is more open.

A compromise between the two practices would be to cut the mouthpiece patch in half and install the smaller patch to ensure grip but also allow more tonal response, although the jaw would still have to open a bit more.

Some people like to use black electrical tape instead of a specifically designed patch. I do not recommend this, as the taste is unpleasant and the tape might contain harmful ingredients that are unsafe for consumption. Additionally, the adhesive on this tape can soften and slip early on.

Here are additional ways to use patches on the mouthpiece:

- No-bite trainer: Cutting small rectangular or half-moon shaped pieces and placing them on either side of the reed creates an elevated surface that is flush with the reed (illustration 2). Playing with these helps prevent biting because the new temporary "elevators" keep the teeth off the reed. This should be used only as a training device.
- Ligature antislip: Install a patch over the mouthpiece's logo stamping to prevent the ligature from slipping upward (illustration 3).
- Upper teeth position trainer: To avoid taking in too much upper mouthpiece, install a half patch slightly away from the mouthpiece tip to stop the upper teeth from sliding down. The upper teeth will rest on the unpatched mouthpiece tip (not illustrated).

Creative ways to use mouthpiece patches on clarinet parts other than the mouthpiece are discussed in Quick Tip 40: Antislip Thumb Patch.

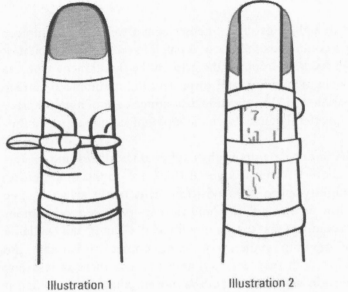

Illustration 1   Illustration 2   Illustration 3

QUICK TIP 40: ANTISLIP THUMB PATCH

Clarinet mouthpiece patches are useful, especially to prevent the upper teeth from slipping and to protect the mouthpiece from sharp teeth. They can also be placed on the mouthpiece's logo to prevent slippage of the ligature.

I also found that placing a mouthpiece patch on the wood surface underneath the thumb rest improves the stability of the right thumb. Since the patch offers added friction and cushion, the player's grip can be relaxed and the right-hand fingers can move more freely. This increases confidence, which allows the clarinetist to concentrate on playing rather than worrying about whether the instrument will slip out of position.

A good brand to use for this purpose is Yamaha Mouthpiece Patches, medium size, 0.5 mm thick (see part A of the following illustration). This product's surface sticks to the thumb, resulting in the clarinet feeling lighter. I experimented with holding the instrument sideways or at an angle with and without the patch, and the difference is significant. The instrument did not budge with the patch on, and it slipped right off my thumb without the patch.

I wholeheartedly recommend the use of the nonslip thumb patch. The result is well worth the temporary concern over sticking an inexpensive patch on a beautiful and luxurious piece of wood. For increased stability, an additional mouthpiece patch may also be placed underneath the thumb cushion.

Patches eventually wear out and come off and can easily be replaced. When necessary, simply remove the old patch, clean the surface by rubbing the extra glue off with your thumb, and affix a new patch.

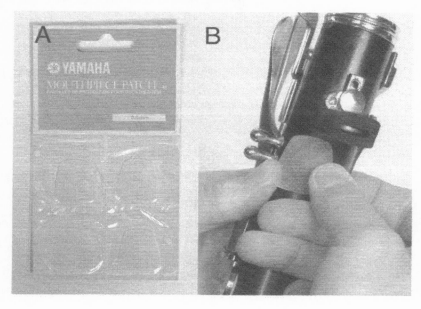

QUICK TIP 41: POSITIONING YOUR REED

As mentioned in Secret 40: Express-Speed Reed Balancing in my previous book, *Clarinet Secrets*, one way to adjust reeds is by scraping the right and left sides with reed rush until both sides are balanced. Balancing reeds with reed rush is a quick, practical, and inexpensive method when pressed for time, such as in the middle of a rehearsal. I found that before applying this technique, one preliminary quick step can be taken that involves no tools or scraping whatsoever.

Well-balanced reeds respond evenly with a clear tone and minimal squeaking. To find out whether your reed's sides respond evenly, play the left and right sides separately. This is done by slightly twisting the mouthpiece to the right and then left while playing, therefore blocking one side's vibration while producing a sound with the opposite side. While comparing each side's sound and response, one side might feel more resistant than the other. Before scraping your reed with reed rush or a reed knife, slightly push the reed to the side and test the reed. If the left side is too hard, push the reed to the right, as illustrated below, and vice versa. After comparing both sides, determine if your reed response has improved enough so you will not need to make any permanent adjustments with reed rush or a knife.

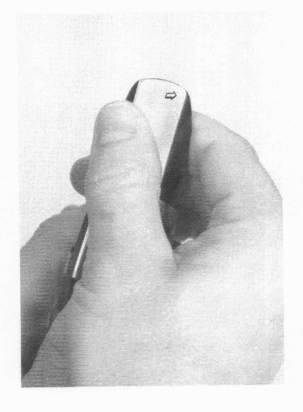

QUICK TIP 42: HOW TO USE A REED CLIPPER

A reed clipper is a handy tool to make the most out of soft reeds. It is used to trim the tip of a reed to remove imperfections and make it harder. I recommend the old classic model made by Cordier because it is sturdy and it is designed for right-handed clipping (see A in photo below). The Rigotti trimmer is more affordable and works well for left-handed users; however, it is less sturdy.

The reed clipper has a fastener that secures the reed onto the flat surface and a screw or knob that precisely positions the reed for trimming. Once the reed is properly positioned, a small lever is pushed, which clips off a sliver of cane from the tip. For best results, only a tiny amount of cane should be clipped.

Steps to clip a reed:

1. Unclip the lever and place the reed onto the flat part of the clipper. Close the fastener.
2. Turn the clipper around so you can see the reed tip and turn the screw either way until the reed slides just above the tip of the reed clipper's blade.
3. Push the lever until you hear a click and remove the reed from the clipper.

Using a clipper is likely to either save or ruin your reed. Therefore, be sure you are willing to take the risk and are not too attached to the reed. It is best to practice using the clipper with a few old reeds before attempting to use it on a potentially good reed.

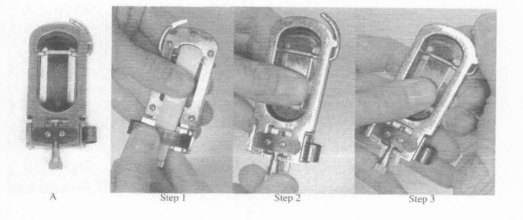

A   Step 1   Step 2   Step 3

QUICK TIP 43: MAKING REEDS LAST LONGER

An interesting question is whether or not reeds should be soaked in water or in the mouth before playing. I believe it is best to soak reeds in water for the following reasons:

1. Saliva contains digestive enzymes that can break down reed fibers and make them age faster.
2. Water is thinner than saliva and can penetrate the reed pores faster and more evenly.
3. It is healthier to soak the reed in clean water rather than putting potentially unhygienic reeds in the mouth repeatedly.
4. Many reeds can be simultaneously soaked in water.

New reeds should be soaked for only a minute or two because the cane pores are open and absorb water quickly. Since pores in older reeds become clogged or flattened, they should be soaked for three to five minutes, depending on age. Avoid over-soaking the reed. If the reed becomes dark and transparent, it is waterlogged and will not vibrate or respond adequately. Always soak reeds at room temperature and in clean water.

When soaking several reeds in a glass of water, remove them and pat them on a paper towel individually to remove excess water. Once the reed is on the mouth-

piece, avoid rubbing it with the palm side of your fingers to prevent any greasy residue from penetrating the reed. Instead, use the back of the index finger when touching reeds. Saliva and skin residue will form a dry crust that will impede reed vibration and shorten its life span, so always rinse your reeds with clean water once you are finished using them for the day.

Keeping the pores clean and open can extend the life of a reed. Pores are the openings into the cane's vascular system, which consists of tiny tubes. Hollow tubes vibrate best, so if they become clogged or rubbed flat, they automatically lose some of their capacity to vibrate. The drawing on page 66 represents an artist's rendition of reed pores. The pores allow water to be absorbed evenly, and can be regarded as miniature vibrating tubes.

QUICK TIP 44: REED RUSH QUALITY CONTROL

Reed rush (also referred to as Dutch rush) is a small, thin, hollow plant with an abrasive surface that is used by clarinetists to scrape and adjust reeds. The plant usually grows along ponds, rivers, streams, or riverbanks, and is harvested, cut, and dried. Techniques on how to use reed rush are described in Secret 40: Express-speed Reed Balancing in my previous book, *Clarinet Secrets*.

A few companies harvest, prepare, and distribute reed rush. My favorite brand is Leblanc because their pieces are usually cut evenly and boxed in a protective, flat, clear container (see photo below). The best pieces will be dark sage green, have a perfectly round and rigid cylindrical shape with clean edges, and be large enough in diameter to have contact with a significant amount of reed surface (see illustration below, "Good").

Unfortunately, reed rush is sometimes sold in soft plastic bags and dried incorrectly, resulting in uneven pieces that are not trimmed or are too small to be effective. These pieces are often very dark and spotty, curved, too thin, and flat (see illustration below, "Defective").

Choosing high-quality reed rush is financially judicious and will ensure a better outcome when working on your reeds.

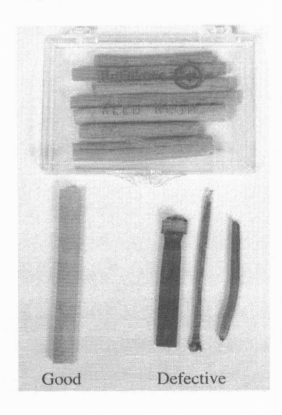

Good   Defective

QUICK TIP 45: HOMEMADE REED RUSH

As mentioned in Quick Tip 44: Reed Rush Quality Control, reed rush (also called Scouring Rush, Horsetail, or *Equisetum hyemale*) is an inexpensive and effective tool used to fix clarinet reeds. The hollow stems are long and straight, measuring twenty-four to thirty-six inches tall, with rings every three to five inches along the stem, much like bamboo (see illustration A, page 71). The plant has an abrasive surface and was used by Native Americans and early settlers to polish wood and silver. Since the plant grows along small bodies of waters throughout the United States, it is possible to acquire and process our own reed rush rather than to purchase the finished product.

Harvesting and Cutting

The obvious first step to obtain reed rush is to find an area where the plant grows. I have found mini-crops along rivers and creeks while taking walks in the woods in Ohio, as well as along a bike trail in Indiana (see illustration, page 71). The best time to harvest the stems is midsummer, when plants are large. Picking the plant when it is fully grown produces larger pieces that dry more evenly and are more desirable for reed work.

Harvest the plant by cutting the stems with sturdy scissors near the bottom of the plant, taking care not to harm the root for future growth. Avoid picking pieces that have dark spots, as brown fluid might seep out and stain your fingers. Trim the unusable thin top sections and buds.

The first step in processing reed rush is to cut pieces three to four inches long. Cutting the reed rush *after* it is dried can result in cracked edges. The rings are not well suited for reed work, so make the cuts accordingly and discard the ring sections (middle piece, illustration B, page 71). On the other hand, if you want to use as much of the plant as possible and the dimensions allow it, you may leave one ring in the middle (first and third pieces, illustration B) of each section rather than cutting it out.

Drying

The most challenging part of preparing reed rush is getting the stems to remain round and stiff while drying. Reed rush appears to be dry when you pick it; however, freshly cut reed rush contains a surprising amount of moisture. It is best to bake the stems early on before they become wrinkled, soft, and flat. Those pieces will not perform as effectively on the reeds as pieces that are perfectly round and firm.

Reed rush can be dried in a microwave oven or a conventional oven. To use the microwave method, place about a dozen precut reed rush pieces on a paper towel and microwave them in increments of ten seconds at 50–70 percent power. Replace the damp paper towel after each cycle and move the pieces around to allow them to dry evenly. Let the pieces rest for a minute between each heating to allow evaporation.

The method works well; however, it requires constant supervision. A word of caution: This method dries the plant very quickly so leaving it in the microwave too long could result in the reed rush catching on fire. Be careful when handling the heated pieces, as the natural oils and moisture in the plant can burn your hands. Remember to place the reed rush on a paper towel instead of a plate. Using a plate requires more drying cycles because the plant's moisture collects on the plate's surface, making it necessary to wipe it dry it between each cycle.

My preferred method is using a conventional oven. Note that any pieces with rings should be baked in a conventional oven as the sections between the rings will pop apart in a microwave oven. Preset the oven to a low temperature, around 175 or 200 degrees, and proceed when the oven is hot. Spread out two or three dozen precut reed rush pieces on a cookie sheet and bake for 45 or more minutes, depending on the type of oven (electric, gas, convection) and size of stems. Shake the cookie sheet every 10 minutes or so and turn over the pieces with a spatula to accelerate evaporation. Make sure the stems are bone dry before turning off the oven, and use a timer for safety. Do not leave the pieces unattended or forget to remove them from the oven.

Let the pieces sit for twenty minutes, then check for rigidity by gently rolling your fingers around each piece, and discard the ones that break or crack under the pressure of your fingers. Also discard the pieces that remained soft and did not dry properly, as well those that did not retain their round shape.

Both microwave and conventional oven techniques tend to give off a pungent odor for a short time.

Storing

Once your chosen pieces of reed rush are dry and stiff, store them in small, protective containers. When dry, the pieces are ready to be used right away. Remember to share the wealth with your clarinet and saxophone friends and colleagues. They will appreciate the gesture.

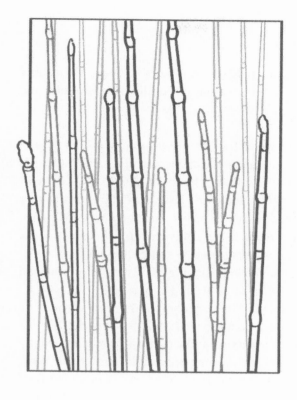 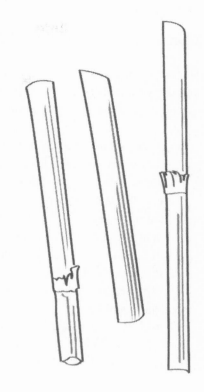

A   B

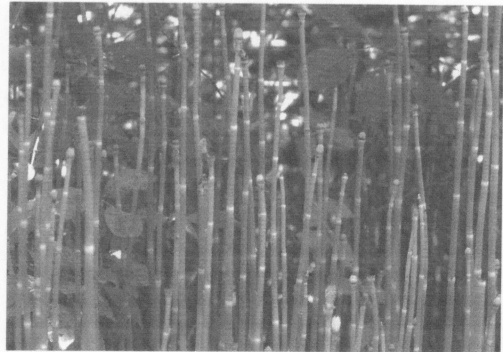

QUICK TIP 46: ROTATING REEDS

An important aspect of maximizing your reeds' potential is to rotate them on a regular basis. Reed rotation systems vary depending on preference, climate, and experience. Here is a quick and inexpensive way to rotate reeds:

1. Soak ten new reeds in lukewarm water for one or two minutes. This allows the water to enter the reed's pores and minimizes warping. If your reeds are not new, soak them for five minutes, as shown in Quick Tip 43: Making Reeds Last Longer. Previously played reeds have closed pores resulting from biting and the dry skin and saliva deposits that tend to clog pores. Water can enter the pores of new reeds more easily than older reeds, so it is important to adjust the amount of soaking time to suit each reed.

2. Place the ten wet reeds on a paper towel, making sure they stay bunched together to prevent them from drying while testing each one.

3. Play each reed for a few minutes and write a symbol on the reed's front side to describe its potential quality. For example, write "G" for "good," "H" for "hard," "S" for "soft," and so on. I sometimes like to draw mini icons on my reeds for quick reference such as ☺ or ♡ on a particularly good reed. Writing on the face of the reed allows for quick retrieval when selecting reeds. If you write on the back of the reed, you will need to remove it from your reed holder once it is stored in order to differentiate the reeds from one another. After all, we prefer to spend our time playing, so minute details add up to save time. During testing, place each reed in order of preference, flat side up (best reed first and worst reed last). At this point, the reeds are separated and start to dry.

4. Once you have rated ten reeds, play them all again to see which ones maintain their playability while they are in the process of drying. Those reeds will be the faithful ones down the road. Play each reed for a few minutes regardless of quality. After playing all reeds twice (once wet and a second time after drying has been initiated), store unwanted reeds in a container for later trial. Undesirable reeds can become great reeds after sitting in a box for several months, so it is a good idea to keep them, not to mention that it increases the return on your investment.

5. Repeat the process the next day, keeping in mind to soak reeds a bit longer if they have been used previously. You might notice your order of preference has changed by the second day. Play each reed for a longer period of time and place your favorite reeds in containers in order of preference. This will allow you to keep track of the best reeds on hand for the next performance or lesson.

6. Try to keep four to eight reeds in your rotation at all times. This way, you will always have playable reeds on hand when needed. Very good reeds can completely change overnight due to variations in temperature and humidity, so keeping at least four reeds will improve your chances of finding a good reed each day.

After a few months of writing on your reeds, you will notice that hard reeds may become easier to play, whereas the soft reeds may be more difficult to play. The lessons you learn through this process will eventually help you understand the tendencies of reeds, as well as improving your reed rotation skills over time.

QUICK TIP 47: TAPE TYPES

It is surprising how many types of tapes can be used for quick minor repairs. The photo below illustrates five kinds of tapes:

A. Black electrical tape: Found in hardware stores, this tape can be applied anywhere on the clarinet's body and blend in because of its color. A few

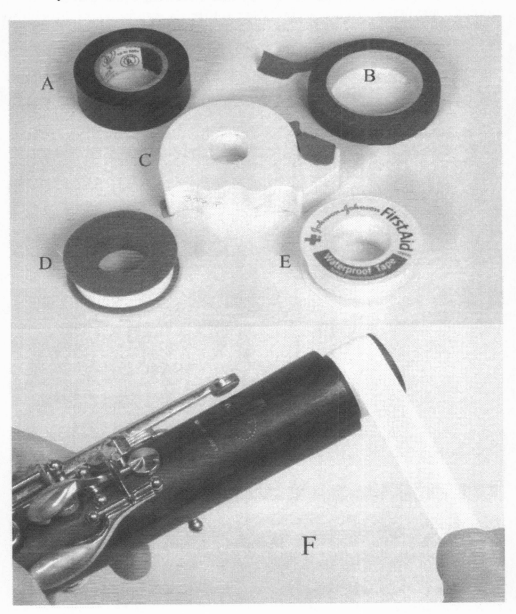

layers can be applied underneath a key to reduce noise or adjust a gap between keys, or placed inside a tone hole to flatten the pitch.

B. Green floral tape: Found in floral shops or hobby stores, this tape can be temporarily applied over a loose tenon joint cork. Apply cork grease over the tape and assemble the joints normally.

C. Thin first-aid tape: Found in pharmacies, this tape can be applied inside tone holes to adjust minor intonation problems or fill in the gap between keys.

D. Plumber's (or Teflon) tape: Found in hardware stores, this tape can be applied temporarily over a loose tenon joint cork (see F). Apply cork grease over and under the tape and assemble the joints normally. It can also be rolled up over the metal thumb rest to prevent the thumb cushion inserted over it from slipping off.

E. Thick first-aid tape: Found in pharmacies, this tape can be applied inside tone holes to adjust significant intonation problems or fill in the gap between keys.

Some of the various kinds of tapes available can be a clarinetist's best friend in both routine and emergency situations. Exploring the possible uses for each one can save the day as well as improve your performance outcomes.

QUICK TIP 48: TAPE IN TONE HOLE

Clarinetists face interesting intonation challenges due to the register hole serving double function with the B♭ throat note. The register tone hole is too large for register notes (therefore they tend to be sharp); however, it is too small to allow the throat B♭ to sound resonant. Closing extra holes when playing throat notes helps darken the tone and lowers the pitch, and refraining from biting helps flatten the register notes' intonation. In some cases, however, a small procedure can help lower the pitch on notes that are usually quite sharp, such as the clarion E (fourth space on the staff). Since a smaller tone hole results in lower pitch, tape can be added in the tone hole to fix the problem.

Before starting, make sure to clean the surface inside the tone hole with a damp cotton swab to ensure adherence. The following steps are illustrated in the photos on page 77.

A. Cut a 1.25-inch piece of white first-aid tape (see photo A). This kind of tape is waterproof and is thick enough to require only one layer. The tape can be trimmed to size once it is applied inside the tone hole. With experience, you will be able to closely estimate the length of tape required to cover the entire tone hole without overlapping. A length of 1.25 inches is a good starting point. If intonation only needs minute correction, use a thinner kind of first-aid tape as shown in photo C in Quick Tip 47: Tape Types.

B. Cut a thin piece that will fit into the tone hole, and trim the jagged edges if applicable (see photo B).

C. With tweezers, apply the trimmed piece of tape into the tone hole evenly, avoiding overlapping (see photo C).

D. Make sure the tape covers the entire surface. This takes a little practice and can be mastered in a few weeks (see photo D).

E. If you prefer the tape to remain invisible, apply black electrical tape as shown in photo A in Quick Tip 47: Tape Types. Since the black tape is thinner, two plies may be needed.

F. If a note is sharp, put the tape in the tone hole immediately below the last finger playing the note. For example, to flatten clarion E, apply the tape in the D hole. To flatten clarion D, apply the tape in the F/C right-hand tone hole (this requires removal of the key).

Obviously, it is much easier to add tape inside a hole that is not covered by a key, however, with a little practice, this can be achieved on most notes. Do not apply tape in very small holes, and only apply tape when a note is extremely sharp even when proper embouchure is used. Once applied to a clean surface, the tape should stay in place for years.

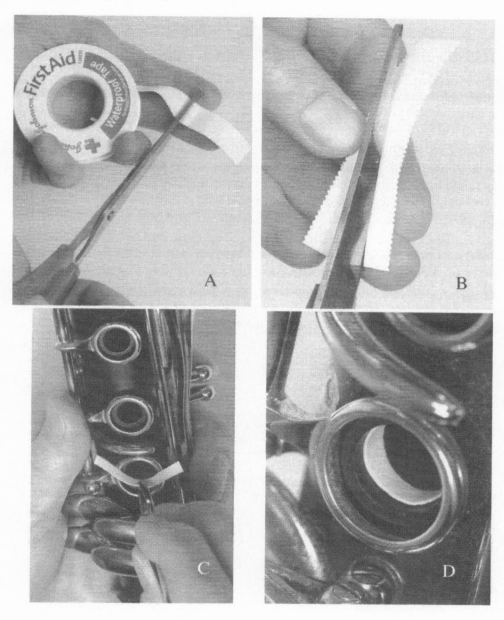

QUICK TIP 49: VALENTINO SYNTHETIC CORKS

I believe in being an innovator.—Walt Disney, American pioneer of animated films

In the past, it took a professional repairperson several hours to replace a clarinet tenon joint cork. The repair equipment needed was a sheet of cork, a razor knife, sandpaper, and contact cement. Some of the necessary repair steps involved cutting the cork to size, gluing it and tying the cork in place overnight, and sanding the cork the next day.

Thankfully, almost anyone can now do the same repair in a few minutes using an innovative synthetic precut cork material made by a company called Valentino and distributed by J. L. Smith & Co. The synthetic corks are easy to install and are more flexible than natural cork. Therefore, they fit better and last longer.

To replace a tenon joint cork, remove the old cork and gently and carefully clean the area with a small screwdriver, blade, or similar tool. Remove the adhesive protective paper from the back of the synthetic precut cork, and tightly wrap the cork around the tenon. Trim off the excess cork and save it for key work. The adhesive behind the cork is extremely effective and the cork will stay in place for years.

Valentino cork products are illustrated below: Key corks in precut shapes (A), and joint corks (B). The joint corks can also be used for mouthpieces, and trimmings can be used for various key cork work.

Synthetic clarinet pads, repair kits, and woodwind supplies are also available. Visit www.jlsmithco.com.

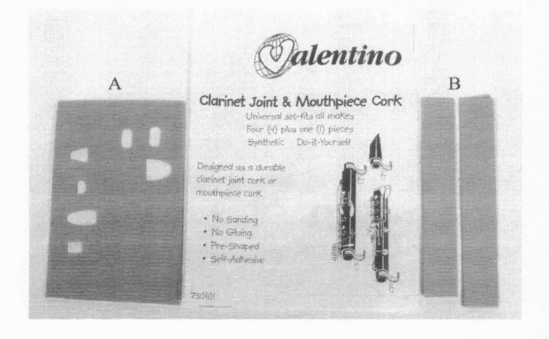

QUICK TIP 50: QUICK-ADVICE BULLETIN
BOARD—REEDS AND EQUIPMENT

- To prevent your thumb cushion from slipping off the thumb rest, apply plumber's Teflon tape around the metal thumb rest and secure the thumb cushion over it.
- To prevent the thumb rest screw (if present) from loosening, apply a small amount of putty on its base.
- Although it is tempting to fault the reed for a less than satisfactory sound, it is important to keep in mind that a clarinetist's job includes preparing and fixing reeds. Reed-fixing skills ultimately enhance your performance success.
- To prevent reeds from warping, soak them in a glass of room temperature water. Soak new reeds for one minute and older reeds for four minutes. Cane pores on older reeds tend to become clogged, inhibiting water infiltration.
- To keep track of your favorite reeds, place small stickers in shapes such as hearts or stars on the plastic reed holder or inside a reed case. Choose different color stickers to identify special characteristics such as concert-ready reeds, practice reeds, or jazz reeds.
- When assembling your instrument, make sure to verify that your forked, one-one fingering (left and right index fingers) seals tightly and that the pad below the left index finger is not leaking. If this fingering does not seal properly, some notes, including the forked E♭/B♭ will either squeak or not respond adequately.
- If a neck strap is needed or preferred, verify that it is the correct length depending on your height and the neck strap ring's position on the instrument. To learn how to install a ring on your thumb rest, refer to Secret 41: Installing an Instant Neck-Strap Ring in my previous book, *Clarinet Secrets*. Apply cork grease regularly to avoid wearing down mouthpiece and tenon corks.
- When putting together your mouthpiece and joints, blow warm air on the greased corks to facilitate assembly.
- To pull apart stuck joints, slightly "crack" them up and down before rotating them right or left.
- When cork grease fails and joints keep getting stuck or will not insert completely, gently sand the inside of the receiving tenon with your index finger. Use very fine grit sandpaper and make sure the inside tenon is free of cork grease beforehand. Avoid excessive sanding by continually checking tightness.

- Use a silk swab to clean your mouthpiece and instrument. Run the swab through the mouthpiece or joints gently and slowly in order to avoid wearing down the mouthpiece's baffle and the joints' inner walls. Insert the swab through the bottom of the mouthpiece to protect the tip and edge rails. Avoid cotton or shammy swabs as they are thicker and more abrasive and can erode inner surfaces over time.
- When trying new reeds, test them by playing a piece of music instead of your usual warm-up pattern. Players tend to subconsciously choose comfortable notes and articulations when warming up; however, the true reed response test comes when patterns are chosen by a composer instead.
- When choosing and breaking in new reeds, remember to play soft dynamics. Most reeds respond adequately when played loudly.
- To flatten a warped reed tip quickly, wet the reed for a few minutes and flatten the wet reed by rolling the hard side of your thumb back and forth over its tip.
- Use powder paper to eliminate sticky pads. Insert the paper gently between the tone hole and pad, close the pad, and press lightly on the pad while slipping the paper off. Repeat if necessary. Make sure to choose a powder paper specifically designed for woodwind pads, as other kinds (such as makeup powder paper) contain excessive amounts of talc and eventually exacerbate the problem. If proper powder paper is not available, thin, glueless, cigarette paper can be used instead.
- Insert a "reward if found" note along with your contact information in your clarinet case in the event you lose your instrument.

CHAPTER 5

Repertoire

QUICK TIP 51: BE THE FIRST TO PRACTICE
SECOND CLARINET ORCHESTRAL PARTS

Clarinetists who aspire to join a symphony orchestra spend years practicing first clarinet parts from the orchestral literature. They find out which works are included on professional orchestra audition lists, study from excerpt books that contain mostly first clarinet parts, and take lessons from accomplished orchestral musicians. All of this is excellent preparation for a principal clarinet position, but what if the job opening is for second clarinet?

If clarinetists focus only on first clarinet parts during their studies they will inevitably be at a disadvantage when a second clarinet position becomes available. It is illogical to prepare for a principal clarinet position in college, yet wait until the last minute to practice for a second clarinet position as a professional. Although most of us aspire to play first chair, many of the opportunities are for second part. Additionally, younger players would gain valuable experience playing second part for several years before moving into a principal position.

Second clarinet audition repertoire lists do include some first clarinet parts (and most often the Mozart clarinet concerto), yet being proactive and mastering second clarinet parts early on is a great way to improve chances of being competitive for such a position.

One problem is that second clarinet parts are hard to find since they rarely appear in pedagogical materials. Check various professional orchestral websites to see if they post PDF files of audition repertoire for the positions of Associate Principal, Assistant Principal, or Second Clarinet. Note that these positions usually include E♭ piccolo clarinet duties (see Quick Tip 52: E♭ Piccolo Clarinet Orchestral Audition Preparation).

Other sources of second clarinet parts are university orchestral libraries, community and professional orchestral libraries, and most recently, *The Orchestra*

Musician's CD-ROM Library. The CD-ROMs include complete first and second clarinet parts, and they are available at orchmusiclibrary.com. Some second clarinet parts are included in orchestral excerpt books such as *Orchestral Excerpts from the Symphonic Repertoire for Clarinet* in eight volumes, compiled by Robert McGinnis and Stanley Drucker (International) and *Orchester Probespiel: Test Pieces for Orchestral Auditions for Clarinet*, edited by Heinz Hepp and Albert Rohde (C. F. Peters). The latter includes excerpts for auxiliary instruments (piccolo and bass), and both titles include some second clarinet parts for pieces such as Ravel's *Daphnis et Chloé* (Suite no. 2) and the Scherzo in Mendelssohn's *A Midsummer Night's Dream.*

Playing second clarinet in an orchestra is not for everyone. It requires special skills like respectful cooperation, willingness to take criticism, flexibility, and ability to match the principal clarinet in style, tone, and intonation. Second clarinet parts typically include more rests than first parts so it is important to develop a long attention span when counting rests. This certainly will be appreciated if the first clarinet inadvertently loses count.

Lastly, playing second clarinet entails humility to accept that most often the credit and accolades will be directed toward the principal player. The upside is that there is a lot to be said for being part of it all with virtually none of the solo stress. Also, in contrast with other woodwinds such as the flute, oboe, and bassoon, the clarinet is the most suited to play "second" because of how easily the low register responds on the instrument. For these reasons I see the second clarinet chair as one of the best seats on stage.

The second clarinet excerpts most often found on audition lists are:

Bartók: *Concerto for Orchestra, Miraculous Mandarin Suite,* and *Symphonies no. 8* and *9*
Beethoven: *Symphonies no. 2* (2nd movement), *5, 6, 8,* and *9* (3rd movement)
Berlioz: *Symphonie fantastique* (3, 4, 5)
Brahms: *Piano Concerto no. 2* (3), and *Symphonies no. 2* (4), 3 (2), 4
Britten: *Young Person's Guide to the Orchestra*
Bruckner: *Symphony no. 7*
Debussy: *La mer*
Mahler: *Symphony no. 4*
Mendelssohn: *Midsummer Night's Dream, Fingal's Cave Overture* (*Hebrides*), and *Symphonies no. 3* and *4* (2, 4)
Mozart: *Symphony no. 39* (1, 2, 3)
Rachmaninoff: *Symphony no. 2* (3)
Ravel: *Daphnis et Chloé* (Suites no. 1 and 2), and *Rhapsodie espagnole* (cadenza)

Rimsky-Korsakov: *Scheherazade* and *Rapsodie Espagnole*
Roussel: *Bacchus & Ariane no. 2*
Shostakovich: *Symphonies no. 1* and *5* (3)
Smetana: *Moldau*
Strauss: *Till Eulenspiegel* and *Don Juan*
Stravinsky: *Firebird* (1919) and *Petrouchka* (1947)
Tchaikovsky: *Symphony no. 5* (1st movement, opening)

QUICK TIP 52: E♭ PICCOLO CLARINET
ORCHESTRAL AUDITION PREPARATION

One way for a clarinetist to maximize performance opportunities is to become proficient on the E♭ piccolo (or sopranino) clarinet. Great parts have been written for the instrument in the wind symphony and military band repertoire. In addition, important E♭ clarinet solos are found in the orchestral repertoire and while a significant portion of orchestral music written before the early 1900s included D clarinet parts, most have been transposed for E♭ clarinet.

The process of preparing for an orchestral audition is complex, and the proper steps need to be taken to increase chances for a successful outcome. Essential steps include acquiring the appropriate sheet music and recordings, studying with a qualified teacher, planning a rigorous practice schedule, playing your audition material for teachers and colleagues, and researching details about the audition process, audition space, committee procedures, and schedule.

About a dozen excerpts are considered to be standard for E♭ clarinet orchestral auditions. The most frequently requested are *Symphonie fantastique* (5th movement) by Berlioz, *Boléro, Daphnis et Chloé (Suite no. 2)*, and *Piano Concerto in G Major* by Ravel, *Symphonies nos. 5* and *6* by Shostakovich, *Till Eulenspiegel* by Strauss, and *The Rite of Spring* by Stravinsky. Other excerpts include *El Sálon México* by Copland, *Symphonies nos. 1, 6,* and *9* by Mahler, *Symphony no. 7* by Shostakovich, and *Also Sprach Zarathustra* and *Heldenleben* by Strauss.

Some works require doubling on B♭, A, and C clarinets, so it is important to acquire or borrow these instruments or to be prepared to transpose some sections. Aspiring professionals will usually purchase a set of B♭ and A clarinets early on; however, they may wait many years before investing in additional instruments. Serious clarinet students may eventually choose to acquire C and D clarinets, but due to the considerable cost, many clarinetists prefer to transpose when necessary.

One example of a transposed part is *Till Eulenspiegel* by Richard Strauss, which was originally written for D clarinet. In the past, some handwritten parts transposed for E♭ clarinet were floating around the audition circuit; however, a professionally printed part is now available in Peter Hadcock's *Orchestral Studies for the E♭ Clarinet*, published by Roncorp. This excellent resource contains most of the main orchestral excerpts for E♭ clarinet and includes helpful performance and fingering annotations by the author.

Other orchestral excerpt books include *Strauss Orchestral Excerpts Volume 3 for Bass, E♭ and D Clarinets*, published by International, and three comprehensive volumes compiled and edited by French clarinetist Jacques Merrer, entitled *Orchestral Excerpts for Sopranino Clarinet*, published by International Music Diffusion. Currently E♭ clarinetist with the Lille Orchestra, Merrer plans to publish two additional volumes in the future.

I interviewed Jonathan Gunn, Associate Principal and E♭ Clarinet with the Cincinnati Symphony Orchestra, and he offers the following advice.

1. Acquire the best instrument you can find. Also find a setup that is comfortable to play and not too stuffy. Often, E♭ novices get old instruments that are in poor shape and very difficult to play.
2. Experiment with many different equipment combinations (mouthpiece, barrel, ligature, reeds). If you cannot get E♭ reeds to work well, you may get better results by cutting off the butt end of a B♭ reed.
3. Learn every possible alternate fingering and be ready to use them. If you have trouble finding an in-tune fingering for a particular passage, try to create your own.
4. Train your ear and remain very flexible with pitch. It is crucial to be able to quickly adjust intonation.
5. Be able to vary the sound of the instrument. The E♭ clarinet does not always have to sound bright and shrill. Experiment with your tongue position. You may find that a tongue position that is ineffective for B♭ clarinet works very well on E♭.
6. Think small with your fingers. Use smaller movements and be extra careful to have a natural, curved finger position. When the fingers are flat it is especially difficult to cover the relatively small tone holes correctly.
7. Plan practice time carefully and avoid over-practicing immediately before an audition. Intense last-minute E♭ practicing can result in excessive biting and a sore bottom lip.
8. Air support is crucial, so do not back off when you are unsure.
9. Be careful not to hunch over just because the instrument is small. Poor posture restricts airflow and creates tension while playing.
10. Above all else, be confident. Lack of confidence and the E♭ clarinet do not mix well.

QUICK TIP 53: BASS CLARINET ORCHESTRAL AUDITION PREPARATION

Another way for a clarinetist to maximize performance opportunities is to become proficient on the bass clarinet. Increasing your versatility will make you a more marketable musician, opening doors such as bass clarinet auditions and increased chances to perform as a substitute bass clarinetist. Serious clarinet students would benefit from taking lessons from a professional bass clarinetist.

Edward S. Palanker, bass clarinetist with the Baltimore Symphony Orchestra, offers the following advice.

Few clarinetists own a bass clarinet, so a good way to get more engagements is to acquire one. For orchestral auditions, it is necessary to own a bass clarinet that goes down to low C because there is a good deal of music that requires the added range in the standard orchestral repertoire. Because new bass clarinets are expensive, one should consider purchasing a used instrument. Ask your teacher for assistance in finding one, search online stores' used inventory, or browse on eBay, Facebook, or the online clarinet board test.woodwind.org/clarinet/BBoard.

In addition to the considerable expense of purchasing a bass clarinet, these instruments present some special concerns of which we must be aware. Common instrument maintenance problems include bending of the long rods, bridge keys, and double-octave mechanism. Be sure to take special care when assembling and taking the instrument apart and keep the joints well greased. Depending on personal interest, aspiring professional clarinetists may want to also consider acquiring a number of auxiliary clarinets such as Eb, D, C, basset clarinet, basset horn, and contrabass clarinet.

You can start practicing some easy Bb clarinet etudes and work up to the Rose studies and more advanced books later on. Since many orchestral excerpts are written in bass clef, I suggest using the original cello *Suites* by J. S. Bach so you can become fluent in reading the bass clef. If this repertoire is too advanced, you can begin by using an intermediate bassoon or cello method instead. Additionally, there is a considerable amount of music written for the bass clarinet in A, so it is a good idea to learn to transpose a half-tone lower as well.

If you are considering taking bass clarinet auditions, be mindful that you must also be an accomplished soprano clarinet player. The largest orchestras employ four clarinet players and the bass clarinetist is expected to play the second part at times, especially when the part calls for both, which is a common occurrence. If the orchestra has three players in the section, sometimes the bass clarinetist also serves as the assistant first clarinetist. If the second player is the assistant first, then the bass clarinet player plays second more often. In the smallest orchestras with only two players in the section, it is an advantage if the second player can also play bass, but it is usually not a requirement for the job.

In any case, when auditioning for a bass clarinet job you will be asked to play the first clarinet parts of the standard repertoire and you may also be asked to play some second parts along with the orchestra's principal clarinetist in the final rounds of the audition.

QUICK TIP 54: BASS CLARINET
TECHNIQUE AND ORCHESTRAL EXCERPTS

Technique

Depending on the angle of the neck you might have to hold the instrument at a slight angle for the best effect. Hold the bell between your feet for support if you don't use a neck strap. Find a comfortable height but do not bend your head down to reach the mouthpiece.

Fingerings are the same as on the soprano clarinet except for the lowest notes (different on various models), and the upper register has two sets of fingerings. Use the half-hole and alternate fingerings for the high register. High C♯ and D can be played with or without the half-hole, whereas the half-hole is necessary above the high D (three spaces above the staff). Fingering charts are available online and in bass clarinet method books such as *The Bass Clarinet* by Jean Marc Volta, published by International Music Diffusion.

Orchestral Excerpts

There are about a dozen excerpts that are considered to be standard for bass clarinet orchestral auditions. Some of the most common are *On the Trail* from the *Grand Canyon* Suite by Ferde Grofé, Strauss' *Don Quixote*, *La Valse* by Ravel, and Khachaturian's *Piano Concerto*.

Orchestral excerpt book collections include three volumes of *Symphonic Repertoire for Bass Clarinet*, edited by Michael Drapkin and published by Roncorp; *Difficult Passages and Solos for Clarinet and Bass Clarinet, Books 1 and 2*, edited by Alamiro Giampieri and published by Ricordi; and the Strauss *Orchestral Excerpt Book Volume 3 for Bass, E♭ and D Clarinets*, published by International.

Orchester Probespiel: Test Pieces for Orchestral Auditions Clarinet, edited by Heinz Hepp and Albert Rohde, published by C. F. Peters, contains orchestra and opera excerpts for soprano clarinet, D and E♭ clarinets, and bass clarinet as well as a few second clarinet excerpts.

Additionally, there are CD-ROM collections entitled *The Orchestral Musician's CD-ROM Library Vol. 11 for Clarinet: Wagner: Part 1*. It includes complete E♭ and bass clarinet parts on CD-ROM in PDF format. *Vol. 11* contains six orchestral works by Wagner and his early operas, and *Vol. 12* contains six of Wagner's later operas.

QUICK TIP 55: BASS CLARINET METHOD BOOKS

Bass clarinet method books include *The Bass Clarinet Method*, by Jean-Marc Volta, published by International Music Diffusion in 1996. This bilingual (French and English) 119-page method is authored by the principal bass clarinetist of the French National Orchestra. The book is beautifully put together and very detailed. It covers important topics such as French and German notation, standing and sitting practice positions, breathing and tone exercises, articulation, extreme low and high registers, orchestral excerpts, and includes comprehensive fingering charts.

Another bilingual bass clarinet book (in Spanish and English) is entitled *Studies for Bass Clarinet*, by Pedro Rubio, who arranged eighteenth- and nineteenth-century etudes for bass clarinet, basset horn, basset clarinet, or contrabass clarinet. Volume 1 includes twenty-five progressive studies for the first register down to low C (although alternate passages are written for instruments going to low E♭ only), and Volume 2 includes thirty progressive studies in the German notation system. Both volumes are published by Música Didáctica.

Bass Clarinet Scale Book, by Martin Arnold (second edition), published by Aztecpress, contains two-octave scales and various scale patterns in both treble and bass clefs for the low E♭ and low C instruments, as well as exercises focusing on the low notes for the low C instrument.

Rhythmical Articulation (for bass clef instruments), by Pasquale Bona, selected and transcribed by William D. Fitch, published by Carl Fischer, includes the bass clef edition with Parts II and III from the original forty-one etudes. This is useful for bass clarinetists who want to work on their bass clef skills.

William E. Rhoads compiled several books for bass clarinet, such as *Advanced Studies from Julius Weissenborn Adapted for Alto and Bass Clarinets* that includes thirty-four studies from the well-known Weissenborn bassoon studies; *Baermann for the Alto and Bass Clarinet*, which is an adaptation of *Division 3* of the very well-known clarinet method by Baermann that consists mostly of scales and arpeggios, and *35 Technical Studies for Alto or Bass Clarinet* that includes a variety of useful exercises for low clarinets including studies on crossing the break, articulation, little fingers, and chords. These books are published by Southern Music Company.

Clarinetists will discover a whole new world of performance opportunities and musical experiences by adding bass clarinet to their skills. An experienced bass clarinet teacher can help you select repertoire, equipment, mouthpiece, and reeds, and give you the edge you need to succeed in your new endeavor.

QUICK TIP 56: JAZZ CLARINET

The clarinet has an important place in the history of jazz, thanks to the historic big bands of Benny Goodman and Artie Shaw in the 1930s and 1940s; Pete Fountain in the 1950s, 1960s, and 1970s; and present-day masters such as Eddie Daniels. Classical clarinetists can greatly enhance their musical expression by adding jazz to their training.

Although one might choose to play classical music almost exclusively, there will come a time when knowledge of the jazz style will be necessary. Perhaps a wind quintet will decide to add a jazz-style piece to their program. Since a quintet includes instruments that traditionally focus on classical repertoire (flute, oboe, bassoon, and horn), presumably the clarinetist will lead the rehearsals for this type of music. Additionally, orchestral works such as Gershwin's *Rhapsody in Blue* or Malcolm Arnold's *Second Clarinet Concerto* require clarinetists to perform in the jazz style.

Saxophonist Dr. Dave Camwell of Simpson College (Iowa) offers the following advice.

Articulation

One of the most important aspects of the jazz idiom is articulation. While classical music primarily features on-the-beat tonguing patterns, jazz (swing, bebop) typically utilizes off-the-beat tonguing patterns. An effective way to start practicing this style is with an eight-note scale pattern such as the example below. Your tonguing should be legato. Work to apply this general articulation concept to most lines you encounter in swing-style jazz.

Jazz Off-Beat Articulation

Another concept is note ghosting. This serves to essentially whisper certain notes in jazz phrases. Ghosting is produced by pulling the jaw slightly back from the mouthpiece while reducing the airflow or by leaving the tongue on the reed.

Here is an example of how to apply ghosting to a typical line of swung eighth notes:

By using ghosting in addition to off-beat articulation, you will create a phrase that is authentic to the jazz style. As in classical music, subtlety in musical effects helps turn a good performance into a great one.

Improvisation

Improvisation is the core of all jazz music. With some basic skills, anyone can develop their uniquely creative musicianship in an exciting and fulfilling way. A plethora of resources on improvisation are available, which can make for an overwhelming and intimidating experience. My suggestion is to purchase the old classic, *Patterns for Jazz*, by authors Jerry Coker, Gary Campbell, Jimmy Casale, and Jerry Greene. This book explains many theoretical concepts and, most importantly, provides extensive exercises to develop motivic ideas in all keys. This is an essential step in learning how to internalize scale/motive/key relationships in a way that is accessible to the beginner, yet progressively challenging as you develop your skills.

Additionally, professional jazz musician Jim Snidero has an excellent series of books entitled *Jazz Conceptions*. Each book contains a play-along CD. In the clarinet version, highly regarded jazz clarinetist Ken Peplowski performs each of the written etudes, which is useful to help match jazz style and articulation. Each track is then repeated without the artist to allow you to try your own improvisational ideas as a soloist with the rhythm section.

Other play-alongs such as the Jamey Aebersold series can also be very useful, but do not include a featured instrumentalist on the recordings. These recordings and methods may be better suited to more advanced players.

Additional essential steps to improve improvisation include transcribing your favorite melodies and solos, studying with an experienced jazz musician, and playing with others. Many colleges and adult musical organizations offer combo programs and camps that are designed for students of all ages who want to develop their musicianship in this area.

Most importantly, authentic jazz cannot be learned out of a book, so it is imperative to listen to the masters and study recordings of improvised solos. Jazz is a demanding art form, but the rewards of learning this music are worth the effort.

QUICK TIP 57: WOODWIND DOUBLING

A great way to multiply professional performance opportunities is by becoming a woodwind doubler. Clarinetists interested in increasing their marketability and playing myriad musical styles may want to consider studying other woodwind instruments such as saxophone, flute, and oboe. Naturally, this requires a great deal of dedication on each instrument as well as a significant monetary investment. Also, it requires the study of techniques that might not be used on clarinet such as diaphragm vibrato, double reed making, or learning different styles of music such as baroque and jazz.

Clarinetist/saxophonist Dr. John Cipolla, Associate Professor of Music at Western Kentucky University and Broadway musician in New York City for twenty-five years, offers the following advice.

At the core of a doubler is someone who sincerely likes playing each instrument as well as various styles of music, and one who can accept being a section player rather than a soloist. The best doublers are very detail-oriented people. Simply knowing how to play each instrument is not sufficient to succeed as a doubler. One must devote years of intense preparation and acquire the best possible equipment.

Equipment

Doublers need top-of-the-line instruments. Eventually, this may also mean purchasing auxiliary instruments such as piccolo, E♭ and bass clarinets, and various saxophones. This translates into a sizable financial commitment, but it can make the difference between your name landing on top of the call list or not.

Know your mouthpieces. Have a variety of mouthpieces that will suit different types of music, especially saxophone mouthpieces for jazz and classical. Precise intonation and clarity of response are difficult to maintain as a doubler because of the embouchure changes between instruments. Good equipment will help you get the most out of your abilities.

Reeds tend to dry out when an instrument rests on the stand for fifteen to twenty minutes at a time. Therefore, it is very important to soak the large reeds (saxophones, bass clarinet) for at least ten minutes before the performance. Arrive at least an hour early to set up instruments and to allow for any delays. Preselect and presoak your reeds before you arrive at the engagement. Warm up before arriving at the performance, and keep any reed adjusting and warming up very quiet once on site. Oftentimes, musicians are not rehired because they warm up with a full-volume concerto, disregarding the stage crew and other musicians who have plenty to do before the performance.

Most popular music ensembles are quite loud, even if they are not amplified, and many professional woodwind doublers who play in such groups experience some hearing loss. Therefore, it is imperative to learn to play with hearing protection. Buy foam or custom-molded musicians' earplugs that enable you to hear while you are playing. The next important step is to use earplugs while practicing so that you can get used to the difference in perceived sound.

Pre-professional Training

I recommend that students begin by mastering one instrument before moving on to others. When the time comes to learn other instruments, study each instrument with a professional teacher and practice each one for a minimum of one year (three to five hours of practice per day). This intensive preparation will enable you to sound as if each instrument is your primary instrument.

Performing Opportunities

Seek out small and large ensemble performance experiences. Ensembles offer doublers opportunities to hone their skills in the areas of style, rhythm, tuning, and blending. A great way to meet potential teachers is to join the local musicians union in your area and call some more established members in the directory and ask if you can take a lesson with them. This will give them an opportunity to hear you and ultimately recommend you for gigs.

Each performance is an unspoken audition for the conductor and other players who might recommend you for other jobs. Always arrive as prepared as possible. This means both specific preparation (learning the actual part) as well as the continual daily practice that raises your basic skill level each week.

Play recitals and chamber music on each instrument at local libraries, churches, and schools for experience in a nonprofessional setting.

Practicing

Practicing as a doubler must be frequent and consistent. Develop warm-up routines that get your air, fingers, and tongue moving in a reasonably short time. It can be a challenge to find enough hours during the day to practice multiple instruments, so it is of the essence to manage your practice sessions wisely. Practice in very short segments (five to ten minutes) and plan what you will accomplish in each one. The accumulation of small practice sessions will eventually add up and result in raising your basic level of playing on a consistent basis.

Some recommended textbooks are as follows: clarinet—*Vade Mecum* by Jeanjean; flute—*On Sonority: Art and Technique* by Marcel Moyse; saxophone—*Top Tones* by Sigurd Rascher.

Learn to blend in a section. Much of the music a doubler plays is section music with a few interspersed solos here and there. Learning to blend your sound, rhythm, and style with others is the most valuable asset a doubler can have.

Get experience playing in a jazz band to develop a feel for the jazz rhythms and styles. Listen to recordings and live performers to develop a genuine saxophone sound conception. Additionally, study the baroque style on flute and oboe.

Musicians respect well-trained and well-prepared musicians, even if they are not playing their primary instruments. Your goal as a doubler is to feel like each instrument is your primary instrument through daily and thorough practice.

Doubling is attractive to musicians because there are more opportunities for gigs and for playing a wide variety of music. The best doublers are the ones who continually study and practice their instruments throughout their entire careers.

QUICK TIP 58: MILITARY BAND AUDITIONS

One of the performance career opportunities for instrumentalists is that of a military band musician. The advantages of these positions include tuition support, loan repayment programs, medical benefits, extensive travel, diverse performance venues and repertoire, attractive compensation, government benefits, and better-than-average job security.

Detailed information profiling clarinet sections in the military bands is discussed in the quarterly magazine *The Clarinet* in a column entitled "Clarinetists in Uniform," by Musician First Class, Cynthia Wolverton, of the U.S. Navy Band in Washington, D.C. Previously, the column was written by Staff Sergeant Diana Cassar-Uhl from the West Point Band, north of New York City. To subscribe to *The Clarinet*, visit clarinet.org.

The column focuses on the "premier bands," and gives readers a snapshot of what it is like to play in a military band. Some of the topics include clarinet personnel, concert tours, reviews of solo performances with military band, chamber groups, clarinet symposiums, and freelance work. Each band employs approximately eighteen clarinetists, providing a significant number of opportunities for those who might be interested in a career as a military musician.

I interviewed Dr. Douglas Monroe, Assistant Professor of Clarinet at North Dakota State University, former commander and conductor in the U.S. Air Force Band, and former clarinetist with the U.S. Army Field Band in Washington, D.C., and he offers the following advice.

Each branch of the military has at least one premier band. Five of the eight bands are stationed in Washington, D.C.: the United States Army Band, the United States Army Field Band, the United States Navy Band, the United States Marine Band, and the United States Air Force Band. Other premier bands are the United States Naval Academy Band in Annapolis, Maryland, the United States Military Academy Band in West Point, New York, and the United States Coast Guard Band in New London, Connecticut.

In addition to the premier bands, the Army has major command bands and division bands, while the Air Force, Marine Corps, and Navy have regional bands. The Coast Guard has no regional units, only its premier band.

What sets the premier bands apart from the others is that their leadership has the authority to hire musicians at a higher-than-normal beginning rank (E-6). Under normal circumstances, attainment of this rank would typically require ten to twelve years of service. Because of this pay incentive, these bands attract highly qualified musicians, making auditions very competitive.

Keep in mind that each military band (whether premier or regional) has a distinct mission. Some regional bands primarily serve the base at outdoor ceremonies and parades, while others focus on performing concert tours. Since each military band has its own procedures, audition requirements, and job descriptions, it is wise to investigate the specific opportunity before spending the time, effort, and money to audition. Individuals who are interested in auditioning for a military band should contact the organization by making a phone call well in advance of the audition date. Make sure to get a good idea what your future employer will expect so you can determine the extent to which the job matches your goals and aspirations.

Job Openings

To find out about military job openings, check the American Federation of Musicians' monthly newspaper available through subscription at afm.org, as well as Musical Chairs at musicalchairs.info/jobs, clarinet jobs on Facebook at facebook.com, and My Auditions at myauditions.com. Be sure to have your resume ready, as well as a cover letter and CD recording if required.

Here are some basic questions to ask a prospective military employer:

- Can you describe the military basic training experience?
- What are the job requirements?
- Will this job be mostly musical or are there other responsibilities, such as wartime tasks, to perform?
- What is the proportion of classical music as opposed to popular, show music, and functional military ceremony music performed by this band?

Military Band Audition Preparation

Military bands' websites usually contain information regarding the audition process and a number of them even provide the sheet music online. Some organizations offer the option of signing up to receive e-mail updates on audition information and repertoire. If repertoire information is not posted online, questions can be promptly answered either by calling or e-mailing the specific band for which you are auditioning.

Audition repertoire normally includes one or two solo pieces such as the Mozart *Concerto*, excerpts from the band and orchestral literature, and sight-reading from the band repertoire. Some commonly listed orchestral arrangements and band works are: Bernstein/Beeler: *Overture to Candide*; Bizet: Intermezzo from *Carmen Suite No. 1*, Brahms: *Symphony No. 3 in F, Opus 90* (2nd movement); Dahl: *Sinfonietta*, Gounod/Tobani: Ballet Music from *Faust*; Grainger: *Lincolnshire Posy*; Hindemith: *Symphony in B♭*; Holst: *Hammersmith*; Lalo/Patterson: Overture to *Le roi d'Ys*; Makris/Bader: *Aegean Festival Overture* (cadenza); Mendelssohn: *A Midsummer Night's Dream* (Scherzo); Mozart: *Serenade No. 10 in B-flat, K. 361* (6th and 7th movements); Suppe/Moses-Tobani: *Overture to Morning, Noon and Night in Vienna*; and Verdi/Lake: *La Forza Del Destino*. Some bands also request major, melodic minor, and harmonic minor scales extending the entire range of the instrument.

To further prepare for the audition, it can be helpful to borrow popular band transcriptions, overtures, marches, and various patriotic selections from a college band library. Note that accurate tempo and rhythm are extremely important aspects of military band auditions, and that is it helpful to learn entire pieces rather than only excerpts.

General Military Band Websites
United States Army Bands: bands.army.mil
United States Navy Bands: www.npc.navy.mil/CommandSupport/NavyMusic
United States Marine Corps Bands (this is not an official link, but contains links to all of the Marine Corps bands): dccobra.com/UsmcBand
United States Air Force Bands: www.bands.af.mil

Premier Band Websites
The United States Army Band ("Pershing's Own"): usarmyband.com
The United States Army Field Band: armyfieldband.com
The United States Military Academy Band (West Point): www.usma.edu/band
The United States Navy Band: www.navyband.navy.mil
The United States Naval Academy Band: usna.edu/USNABand
The United States Marine Band ("The President's Own"): marineband.usmc.mil
The United States Coast Guard Band: www.uscg.mil/band
The United States Air Force Band: www.usafband.af.mil

QUICK TIP 59: CLARINET AND ORGAN REPERTOIRE

Sooner or later, most clarinetists will be asked to play for a church service or event with the resident organist. The combination of clarinet and organ is particularly beautiful because both instruments' pipes are cylindrical, making their sounds mesh and intertwine unusually well, not to mention how pleasant it is to play in gorgeous church acoustics. I would like to offer suggestions for clarinet and organ repertoire, especially because very few arrangements are available transposed for B♭ instruments.

If you browse in music stores in larger cities or online, you will find that wedding music often lends itself to all kinds of church performances. There are several wedding album collections for clarinet and piano that can be played with organ instead. Some websites, such as virtualsheetmusic.com/score/WeddingCl.html, offer downloadable sheet music instead of physical books. Similarly, you can purchase sacred music collections arranged for clarinet and designed for church service settings, such as *Sacred Melodies for Clarinet*, compiled by Norman M. Heim and published by Cathedral Music Press. It includes works by Bach, Handel, Mendelssohn, and Fauré, and is available at earfloss.com/clarinet or encoremusic. com (type "sacred" in the search box). Also available is the clarinet book *Sounds of Worship: Solos with Ensemble Arrangements for Two or More Players*, arranged by Stan Pethel (Brookfield Press). It includes twelve hymns to be played either as a soloist or with two or more instruments. Most pieces are easy to moderate in difficulty.

A book containing popular hymns for clarinet and piano is *Great Is the Lord*, arranged by Keith Christopher, and published by Hal Leonard. Although the hymns are quite simple and often lack a development, the accompaniment is rich and beautiful. The clarinet part is mostly in the chalumeau register and is very easy to read and play (see earfloss.com/clarinet).

Sheetmusic.com offers a collection for clarinet and organ called *Encores and Pieces for Clarinet and Organ* that includes eight pieces originally written by J. S. Bach, Handel, Godard, Schumann, Mozart, and Giordani (arr. Pritz-Georg Holy, published by Kunzelmann). Likewise, one can browse at luybenmusic.com to find clarinet repertoire with "other keyboard" that includes several pieces with organ. Luyben also has arrangements of spirituals and various hymns. Some websites specialize in sacred music such as despub.com. Additionally, you can use any of the many collections of classical pieces for young players such as *Album of Classical Pieces for Clarinet and Piano, Vol. 1*, arranged by Stanley Drucker (International). It includes music by Bach, Corelli, Grieg, Leclair, Loeillet, and Mendelssohn.

Trumpet music is another excellent source because it is usually written in B♭ and has a compatible range. For example, there are two volumes of *Songs of Faith* for trumpet and piano, arranged by Bill Holcombe.

Many movements from baroque sonatas for oboe also are good choices because they are easy to transpose due to their comparable range. Baroque works for flute are also suitable since they rarely include the extreme high notes found in classical or romantic flute repertoire. One example is Telemann's *Sonata in C Minor*, arranged for clarinet and piano by Himie Voxman, published by Rubank/Hal Leonard.

Some pieces from the main clarinet repertoire can also work very well, such as *Suite from the Victorian Kitchen Garden* for clarinet and harp by Paul Reade. The harp part can easily be played on organ. Another wonderful source can be slow movements from various clarinet concertos and sonatas such as Charles Camilleri's *Concertino*, Tartini's *Concertino*, arranged by Gordon Jacob, and the ruler of all adagios, Mozart's *Concerto in A, K. 622*. If you do not have an A clarinet for the Mozart Adagio, you can opt to buy an arrangement of this movement for B♭ clarinet published by Neil A. Kjos. The entire concerto is also published in B♭ by Carl Fischer.

Famous "hits" performed on clarinet and organ are: *Pie Jesu* by Fauré, *Canon* by Pachelbel, *Ave Maria* by Schubert, *Ave Verum* by Mozart, *Adagio* by Albinoni, *Wedding March* by Mendelssohn, *Ave Maria* by Gounod, *Air from Suite no. 3*, *Jesu, Joy of Man's Desiring*, and *Wachet Auf* chorale prelude by J. S. Bach. Clarinet arrangements can sometimes be found or you can transpose from available scores or even make your own transcriptions.

Other, more unusual examples of pieces arranged for clarinet and piano that work well with organ are *Sicilienne* by Maria Teresia von Paradis, published by Neil A. Kjos, and *Trois Gymnopédies* by Erik Satie (arr. Jerry Lanning).

It is important to note that you may want to choose an experienced organist who is able to make quick decisions regarding organ stops that are not indicated on piano parts. Also, the organist is usually knowledgeable about different religious seasons and can help you select appropriate repertoire for each one.

Lastly, before committing to perform, make sure to check the organ's intonation as it can vary drastically depending on construction, temperature, and humidity. Sometimes an organ can be much flatter than A = 440 Hz. In these cases, you may have to find a longer barrel and pull it out, as well as pulling out the middle joint and bell. Another possible solution is to play with an A clarinet with a short barrel and firm up your embouchure in order to raise the pitch. On the other hand, during hot weather the organ can be sharp, making the problem even more challenging. You may have to switch to a C clarinet and pull out all joints. Usually, the organ will be in tune but it is wise to confirm beforehand.

I invite you to review the repertoire and hear an audio clip from my *Arias for the Soul* clarinet and organ CD at michelegingras.com.

QUICK TIP 60: SAXOPHONE

Another way for clarinetists to maximize performance opportunities is to become proficient on the saxophone. As mentioned earlier, increasing your versatility will make you a more marketable musician and well-rounded teacher, not to mention that playing the saxophone opens a whole new world of jazz performing venues.

Although the clarinet and saxophone are both single-reed instruments, they are quite different. Understanding these differences is very important in order to achieve the correct sound and style on the instrument.

The most evident differences between classical clarinet and saxophone techniques include the use of vibrato, fingerings, low register response, mouthpiece angle, instrument weight, mouthpiece and reed size, and repertoire.

Although many clarinetists choose to add vibrato to their classical sound, the general tendency is to play without vibrato, whereas classical (and jazz) saxophonists use vibrato almost constantly. Vibrato on single-reed instruments should be executed with the jaw as opposed to the diaphragm or throat. Vibrato technique is discussed in Secret 44 in my previous book, *Clarinet Secrets.*

Because the clarinet bore shape is cylindrical and it has a register key that produces an interval of a twelfth, instead of an octave, whereas the saxophone is conical with an octave key, the fingering differences are significant. Online clarinet and saxophone fingering guides can be found at wfg.woodwind.org and fingering-charts.com. Additionally, the saxophone has pads as opposed to the clarinet's holes, which are more difficult to cover for beginners with small fingers. Another difference caused by the dissimilar bore shapes is that the low notes on the saxophone are significantly more difficult to produce than on the clarinet.

The left hand thumb position is quite different as well because the saxophone has a left thumb rest, whereas the clarinet has a hole and no left thumb rest. Because of this, the saxophonist's left thumb always rests on the plastic thumb plate compared to being positioned a few millimeters away from the clarinet's left thumb hole.

Aside from the soprano saxophone that is similar in shape as the clarinet, the alto, tenor, and baritone saxophones have curved necks that result in the mouthpiece angle being 90 degrees as opposed to 35–45 degrees with the clarinet.

Since saxophones are heavier than clarinets, a neck strap must be used to distribute the weight evenly and to facilitate finger movement.

Because of the above differences, it is important to take saxophone lessons with a professional. Learning to play a different instrument opens doors to new repertoire and new musical genres, such as jazz, and increases marketability as a performer and teacher.

Additionally, playing saxophone in the classical style will allow you to perform orchestral repertoire such as *Pictures at an Exhibition* by Mussorgsky, *Boléro* by Ravel, *Lieutenant Kijé* by Prokofieff, *Rhapsody in Blue* by Gershwin, and *L'Arlésienne, Suite No. 1* by Bizet. The majority of saxophone orchestral excerpts are included in *Vols. 1* and *2* of *The Orchestral Saxophonist* by Bruce Ronkin and Robert Frascotti (Roncorp).

QUICK TIP 61: PLAYING WORLD MUSIC

Investigating unfamiliar territory is a great way to grow as a person and as an instrumentalist. One way to venture outside the norm as a music student is to play world music. An interesting advantage of playing nonclassical music is that it can help one develop into a better and multifaceted classical musician. It allows players to acquire new techniques and become more flexible, versatile, and creative as performers, not to mention that it can eventually increase your marketability as a working musician. Examples of nonclassical styles include klezmer, Turkish (where the clarinet in G is the norm), Greek, Romanian, Bulgarian, Indian, Albanian, Latin, African, jazz, Dixieland, or rock.

Study

Depending on where you live and the availability of resources and venues, there are many paths that can lead to proficiency in world music. A logical first step would be to start attending live world music festivals. Not only will this expose you to various styles performed by world music bands, these events are also the perfect venues for meeting like-minded professional and nonprofessional musicians.

After attending several events and doing a bit or research, you could try to find a mentor who would be willing to either give you lessons or provide tips regarding which recordings to acquire and the appropriate literature to start playing on your own. If you have the good fortune of finding a person who is willing to teach you privately, play together as much as possible and ask if he or she can include you in a few rehearsals or sessions with their own established group.

Once you are off to a good start, keep doing research, reading books and articles, and listen to as many recordings as possible. Play along with recordings of your chosen style once you get comfortable with the new techniques. Playing nonclassical music by ear is imperative in the long run, as most bands play without sheet music.

Forming a Band

After you've gained some proficiency playing this music, you will want an opportunity to perform it with others. One way to form a band is to place an ad in a local newspaper. Inevitably, someone with experience will respond and things can grow from there. You can also use word of mouth publicity, advertise online, and post ads in music schools, cultural and community centers, coffee shops, specialty restaurants, and international food markets. Posting a Facebook group page inviting people to respond can also generate interest very quickly.

Once you find interested people and start working on elementary repertoire by either transcribing pieces from recordings or finding written material yielded by your research, schedule regular rehearsals with your group. Practice and discuss ways to perform each piece and see if some participants are able to play multiple instruments to increase tonal variety in your ensemble. Details such as special dress or attire as well as sound equipment can also be discussed later on. Playing nonclassical music often requires a microphone, so I recommend that clarinetists acquire a double condenser microphone that attaches to the clarinet such as the AMT WS. It can become wireless by attaching the AMT Wi5C clip-on wireless system. Visit birdlandmusic.net or pro-audio.musiciansfriend.com.

Workshops

Do research online to find music workshops or world music camps. One of the links I found when searching world music on Google yielded an interesting Indian music workshop called Atmic Vision in Colorado, atmicvision.com/workshops. htm. While there might not be a clarinetist on faculty at a number of these festivals, all instruments are usually welcome.

Gigs

Once your group has a one-hour set of music ready to go, try to secure engagements in local parks, coffee shops, or schools. Naturally, the first few years will probably yield unpaid gigs; however, you might be surprised what can happen if your group eventually rises to a more advanced level. Then you can also start investigating playing at local music festivals and fairs. Later on, try to attract reviewers to your concerts to improve your marketability.

Recitals

One of the wonderful perks of adding any kind of nonclassical music to your repertoire is that you can start performing a sample of it on your classical programs. Audiences love variety in programming, and classical concerts ending with unusual repertoire are always warmly received.

Once your band has acquired some amount of recognition, you may wish to start commissioning composers to write for you. Depending on your situation, you may even try to write grants to fund these commissions by researching organizations that support diverse cultural ventures. Grant proposals that describe projects involving the fusion of cultures or styles such as classical-Indian or Greek-America might improve your chances of securing funding.

Sooner or later, when you feel your band is ready for engagements, create and post a website to garner interest and invitations. If possible, post audio and video clips to give web surfers a clear idea of what you have to offer. The web is filled with such groups and by doing research and using a little creativity, you can soon be part of the scene as well. Subscribing to world music blogs or web mailing lists is a good way to stay connected and keep up with the latest information.

Playing in a world music band can be a wonderful experience musically and socially. It is a great way to learn about various cultures, languages, and a sure way to make new friends. I always encourage my students to be open minded and experience all kinds of ways to make music. To read a detailed article on how to form a world music band, refer to an article entitled *I Want to Play Klezmer, So How Do I Form a Band?* authored by one of my former graduate students, Will Cicola. It is available online at wcicola.com/writing.html.

QUICK TIP 62: CANDLE 1—TRADITIONAL KLEZMER BAND CLARINET MUSIC

It is no secret that over the years, I have concentrated a significant part of my creative efforts on performing klezmer, which is the traditional Jewish instrumental dance music used for celebrations and gatherings. I perform with a band in which most instruments are amplified. A typical clarinet lead sheet consists of the basic tune in C, so transposition is required for performance on B♭ clarinet. These parts typically do not include ornaments or indicate octave changes, so it is up to the player to add these elements. Traditional klezmer techniques are described in my first book, *Clarinet Secrets*.

Publishers are catching on to the increasing popularity of klezmer bands and offer more and more books written for various instrumental combinations. These books can serve as a basis for what might later become spectacular performances. Depending on each player's experience with this style, instrumentalists can experiment with the addition of appropriate ornamentation, klezmer sound effects, and accompaniment lines. The band can eventually decide as a group which instrument will solo or play a secondary line in each section. The process can be creative and fun, and the only limit is the group's imagination.

The following titles are only a sampling and are intended for players who need scores for their klezmer band. This repertoire is best suited for gatherings and special events as opposed to concert music that would be more appropriate for a formal clarinet and piano recital. Formal klezmer recital repertoire is discussed in the following Candles 2–8.

1. *Kammen International Folio #1 and Folio #9 for Clarinet or Tenor Saxophone*, by J. J. Kammen. The "bible" of this musical genre during the first half of the twentieth century, these dance gig collections were virtually the only clarinet books available in this genre. Since then, they have been surpassed by several other books, yet they are still in use today. The clarinet and piano books are available separately as part of an instrumental series arranged for trumpet, alto saxophone, accordion, violin, and piano. All parts work together and can be played as an ensemble or as solos with piano. The solo part contains harmony lines to be played while another instrument plays the solo line.

2. *Dance Klezmer Style*, by Marvin Rosenberg, contains arrangements in score format for clarinet, trumpet, trombone, and piano. Drums are ad-lib, however, Rosenberg does include basic beat patterns as well as guitar chords. Separate parts can be manually created from the score. This book is distributed by Tara Publications.

3. *The Ultimate Little Big Band All-time Jewish Classics*, arranged by Jud Flato, is a collection of ten arrangements for one or two instrument lines with harmonies and piano accompaniment. The wind instruments and violin can provide harmonic background or countermelody for the lead voice, and each piece includes an instrumental chorus as well. The complete set includes piano/voice, violin/flute, clarinet, trumpet, trombone, and bass. This is published by Tara and is available at tara.com.

4. *World Music: Klezmer, Play-along, Clarinet*, by Yale Strom. This book of relatively easy pieces includes a clarinet part, piano score, and an accompaniment CD. Tracks include full performances of each piece with Norbert Stachel on clarinet, as well as tracks without the clarinet part. Titles include *The Silver Crown* and *Dorohoi Khusidl* by Strom Yale, plus traditional pieces such as *Ma Yofes*, *Romanian Hora*, and *Stoliner Nign*. This is published by Universal Edition World Music. Another book from the same series is *World Music: Israel, Play-along, Clarinet*, by Timna Brauer and Elias Meiri, which includes popular Israeli pieces played by klezmer bands like *Hava Nagila* and *Tchiribim Tchiribom*. Both books are available at amazon.com.

5. *The Klezmer Band B♭ Folio*, by Ken Richmond, includes twelve authentic klezmer arrangements for band, transcribed from the repertoire of the Yale Klezmer Band. The arrangements are scored for any C or B♭ instruments, and also include guitar or piano chords, making it useful for a combination of various instruments. The repertoire includes traditional titles such as *Lebedik Un Freylekh*, *Khassene Tantz*, and *Nokh A Glezele Vayn*. Both books are available separately (the C book is entitled *The Klezmer Band C Folio*). This is published by Tara Publications, available at tara.com and amazon.com.

6. *Dave Tarras, The King of Klezmer: A New Biography with Rare Photos and 28 Melodies*, by Yale Strom. The melodies contained in this book are scored for B♭ and C instruments, along with chords for accompaniment. The book includes over fifty pages describing the life of the legendary klezmer clarinetist.

7. *Mel Bay Easy Klezmer Tunes* by Stacy Phillips is a collection of beginner-level pieces arranged for C, B♭, E♭, and bass clef instruments in a single book. The accompanying CD demonstrates ensemble versions of all the music performed at slow tempos on clarinet, violin, guitar, and bass.

QUICK TIP 63: CANDLE 2—TRADITIONAL KLEZMER CLARINET MUSIC WITH PIANO, BEGINNER LEVEL

Each year, I receive a number of inquiries from classical clarinetists who would like to include klezmer repertoire on their formal recitals, but are unsure of how to proceed without sheet music. Many klezmer books are available, however, the accompaniment parts often consist of little more than chord symbols and are intended for klezmer bands. Accompaniment rhythmic patterns are typically not written out, making the music useful only for those instrumentalists who have previous experience in this style.

Traditional klezmer tunes were passed down through the generations orally. After the creation of the Broadway musical *Fiddler on the Roof* in 1964 and the subsequent revival of klezmer in the 1970s, numerous bands formed and the music has been growing in popularity ever since.

In recent years, publishers began compiling collections of traditional klezmer tunes with basic, but completely written-out piano accompaniment parts. These books are sometimes hard to find, so here are a few titles that are sure to put a fiery finishing touch on any clarinet recital.

1. *The Klezmer Clarinet, Jewish Music of Celebration*, edited by Edward Huws Jones, published by Boosey & Hawkes, and distributed by Hal Leonard, contains sixteen klezmer tunes for clarinet and piano. Six of the pieces are compatible with a separate collection for violin called *The Klezmer Fiddler*. The editor includes performance tips and program notes for each piece. Note that some tunes in this book are in different keys compared to arrangements typically played by klezmer bands.

2. *Five Klezmer Pieces for Clarinet and Piano*, arranged by Alexis Ciesla and Bastienne Lapalud and published by Advance Music, is a collection of five well-known traditional klezmer pieces. Unlike the Edward Huws Jones collection listed previously, the tunes in this book are in the same keys played by traditional klezmer bands, which can benefit clarinetists who plan to eventually join a band.

3. *That's Klezmer* (published by Edition Peters) is for two clarinets and piano by Peter Przystaniak. The first tune, *Hevenu Sholom Alechem*, is a wonderful crowd pleaser. This collection of twelve pieces contains seven traditional klezmer pieces and five new compositions. The arrangements can be played by either one or two clarinets with piano, two clarinets only, or various combinations of instruments (using the enclosed parts for C instruments). The book contains a play-along CD with Irith Gabriely on clarinet and the author on piano.

4. *Selections from Fiddler on the Roof* is written for clarinet and piano, arranged by David Pugh and published by Warner Bros. The clarinet and piano books are available separately and are part of an instrumental series arranged for flute, trumpet, clarinet, alto and tenor saxophone, and trombone. All parts work together and can be played in an ensemble or as solos with piano. Everyone loves *Fiddler* tunes!

5. *Klezmers* for clarinet and piano, arranged by Coen Wolfgram and distributed by De Haske Publications, is a book of twelve short pieces that are moderately easy to play. The clarinet part is written in the chalumeau register and should be transposed one octave higher. The clarinet melodies are written out very simply and performers will need to add their own ornaments. The piano score also includes chord symbols and a short text on klezmer style.

QUICK TIP 64: CANDLE 3—KLEZMER CLARINET
RECITAL MUSIC WITH PIANO, INTERMEDIATE LEVEL

In recent years, composers of "legit" music have added wonderful klezmer-style recital pieces to the clarinet repertoire with fully composed piano parts. These pieces are gaining popularity with performers, so I would like to suggest a few titles that are great additions to intermediate-level classical clarinet recitals.

1. *Four Hebraic Pictures in the Klezmer Tradition* is an arrangement that is probably one of the best-known works for clarinet and piano in this genre. It is a collection of four well-written pieces by three composers, with each piece bound separately. The tunes may be played individually or they can be combined into a suite. The titles are: *The Wedding* by Gregor Fitelberg (in two movements), *Canzonetta (Grandmother's Tale)* and *The Maypole* by Jacob Weinberg, and *Hebrew Dance Op. 69* by Boris Levenson. All are arranged for clarinet and piano by Simeon Bellison, edited by Sidney Forrest, and published by Southern Music Co. *Canzonetta* was recorded by this author on her CD, *Old World Meets New World* (SNE 631).

2. Israeli composer Daniel Galay created two collections of *Klezmer Tunes with a Classical Touch*. Volume 1 comes with a clarinet part (or violin), and a complete piano part. An audio CD (entitled *Klassical Klezmer*) containing all eighteen pieces in this volume was recorded by this author and is available at msrcd.com. Volume 1 is also available for clarinet or violin solo with string orchestra. Three of the pieces were arranged for clarinet choir by Greg Barrett.

3. Volume 2 includes a clarinet part (or violin) and an attached CD recorded by this author. The CD also contains a PDF file of the piano part. The piano accompaniment is quite challenging, so you will need to find an accomplished pianist. Pieces from both volumes may be played in order or combined to create suites of various lengths, depending on the number of pieces chosen. Both volumes are published by OrTav Publications in Israel, OrTav.com. Note that the second piece, *Farfalekh*, is the title tune used in my *ClariNET* videocasts posted on iTunes and YouTube.

4. *Suite Hébraïque no. 1* (1964) by Jewish-Canadian composer Srul Irving Glick contains five short movements totaling about ten minutes. Published by Boosey & Hawkes, it is recorded by this author on her CD entitled *Old World Meets New World*.

QUICK TIP 65: CANDLE 4—KLEZMER CLARINET
RECITAL MUSIC WITH PIANO, ADVANCED LEVEL

The following titles are for advanced players and fit very well within the context of advanced-level formal recitals.

1. My top favorite is called *Sholem-alekhem, rov Feidman!* by Béla Kovàcs. It is part of a series of pieces the composer wrote in homage to Rossini, Strauss, and Gershwin. All these pieces are instant crowd pleasers. *Sholem-alekhem* is a tribute to the "King of Klezmer," Giora Feidman, and is published by Edition Darok.

2. Another terrific piece is *Klezmer Fantasy* by American composer Adam Levowitz and published by Woodwindiana. As with the piece mentioned previously, it contains major elements of klezmer such as a written improvisatory introduction, a medium-tempo, triple-meter *hora*, and a flashy, technical ending. This piece stands out from others in that it has a challenging piano part. Detailed performance notes by this author are included in the score.

3. *El Casot* ("little house") by French composer Daniel Bimbi and published by Emerson is a fun showpiece that captures the elements of flamenco, czardas, and klezmer. It contains many repeated sections that can be physically challenging to play, and therefore players may opt to make some cuts.

4. *KlezMuzik* (1995) by American composer Simon A. Sargon contains a mix of slow and lively and ornamented dance tempos and meters (seven minutes). The work is self-published and is available through VanCott Information Services, Inc.

5. *Three Hassidic Dances* for clarinet and piano were written by Israeli composer Yehezkel Braun in 1978. The score is available at the Israel Music Institute by emailing musicinst@bezeqint.net.

6. *Pastorale variée for Clarinet and Piano, Op. 31b* (1952) by Israeli composer Paul Ben-Haim and published by Theodore Presser Co., is a classic and it consists of a theme with six variations in a range of tempos and styles. The klezmer style is quite subtle in this work.

QUICK TIP 66: CANDLE 5—KLEZMER REPERTOIRE
BY MIKE CURTIS AND MICHAEL KIBBE

In recent years, the klezmer clarinet repertoire has been greatly enhanced by American composer Mike Curtis. His inspiration stems from his transcriptions of the repertoire from the 78 rpm records released in the 1920s by Naftule Brandwein and Davis Tarras, two legendary klezmer clarinetists. The following repertoire contains complete scores that can be easily read by classically trained clarinetists. Naturally, it would be quite helpful to find some recordings by Brandwein or Tarras before attempting the first reading. An excellent source for klezmer recordings is jewishmusic.com.

1. *Ten Klezmer Duos, Vols. 1 and 2.* The first book of clarinet duets contains six traditional and four original klezmer tunes, while the second book contains three traditional Sephardic tunes (containing musical elements of modern day Portugal and Spain), six originals, and one piece by Ray Musiker. Both clarinet parts are equally challenging, although the first part will oftentimes sound more stylistically familiar when played one octave higher. Some long duets are printed on foldout pages to eliminate the need for page turning.

2. *Three Klezmer Trios for Three Clarinets.* The second movement is a traditional medley of Chassidic tunes sandwiched by *Bulgar* and *Freylakh* dance movements.

3. *A Klezmer Wedding for Clarinet Quartet* (three B♭s and bass). This is an original composition by Curtis, but it is written in a traditional style. Already a staple in this genre, the piece opens with the proverbial slow, improvisatory introduction called a *Doina*. This is followed by a *Hora* dance rhythm (in 3/8 meter), and an ending with two more dances, *Chusidl* (lively duple meter), and *Freylach* ("happy song"), giving it its typical klezmer sparkling ending. Curtis annotated the music with mordents, trills, and ornaments, making it easier for klezmer novices to perform it in a convincing way. A great audience grabber, it is fun to play, and each part has interesting challenges. An arrangement is also available for woodwind quartet (flute, oboe, clarinet, and bassoon) and wind quintet (quartet plus horn).

4. *Klezmer Triptych for Clarinet Quartet* (two B♭s, alto, and bass). These are terrific traditional tunes in three movements that can be performed individually.

5. *Global Tour for Clarinet Quartet* is a journey through four styles of music: funk, jazz, klezmer, and tango. It is also available for clarinet choir (MSS). I recommend any books by Mike Curtis (most are published by Advance Music). Curtis is doing performers a great service by providing much needed written material and his expertise in klezmer is evident in all of his publica-

tions. One can only hope to see more from him in the coming years. *Mazel tov!*

Another prolific contemporary American composer and arranger of klezmer clarinet repertoire is Michael Kibbe. Many of Kibbe's klezmer works are published by Woodwindiana.

1. *Klezmer Memories, Op. 169* is for three clarinets and bass clarinet. Each part has four pages. The first clarinet is assigned the majority of solo lines, with a few solos in the other parts. The 6'42" quartet opens with a short traditional written improvisation, followed by various dance sections and a fast, whirling, and crowd-pleasing ending.
2. *Serenade, Op. 131* for two clarinets contains seven brief movements that are mostly traditional dance forms from various countries. The last movement is a Jewish *Hora*. Fun to play, both parts are busy but not too technically demanding. The flashy *Hora* is an audience pleaser.
3. *Shtetl Tanzen* for three clarinets (E♭, B♭, and bass) covers two movements that are original compositions in the style of traditional klezmer. It opens with the customary slow, improvisational *Doina* and includes the typical dance movements such as the *Hora*, *Polka*, and *Bulgar*.
4. *Folk Song #1 (Klezmer) for Wind Quintet* (flute, oboe, B♭ clarinet, bassoon, and horn) is an arrangement of anonymous traditional klezmer tunes.
5. *Chassidic Song for Wind Quintet* is also an arrangement of anonymous traditional klezmer tunes.

QUICK TIP 67: CANDLE 6—KLEZMER RECITAL
REPERTOIRE FOR CLARINET AND SMALL ENSEMBLES

Several klezmer-style works are available for wind quintet, clarinet quartet, clarinet trio, and mixed chamber groups. I recommend the following works:

1. *Klezmer Dances for Woodwind Quintet* is arranged by Gene Kavadlo, adapted for wind quintet by Adam Lesnick, and published by International Opus. This suite of four contrasting klezmer dances includes *Freylekh* (a lively circle dance), *Khosidl* (Chassidic slower dance in duple meter), *Kolomeyke* (brisk dance from the Ukraine), and *Kamariska* (lively dance resembling a polka). Kavadlo includes two pages of historical notes and performance instructions in the score, and many ornaments are notated in the solo parts. All four movements are fun, very well arranged, and feature a prominent clarinet part, which is appropriate since the clarinet is the standard "star" wind instrument in a klezmer band.

2. *Rhapsody on a Chasidic Tune for Wind Quintet*, by Samuel Baron, edited by Carol Baron, and distributed by Oxford University Press, is a short potpourri of music by the Chasidic (literally meaning "loving kindness"), which is a group of Orthodox Jews who adhere to a specific philosophy emphasizing spirituality of religion based on the teachings of Rabbi Eliezer, who founded the movement in the eighteenth century. The work includes several fast and slow tunes played in turn by each instrument, concluding with a fast, typical audience-wowing klezmer ending.

3. *Klezmer Music for Woodwind Quintet* by Donald Draganski has three very well-written movements entitled *Hassidic Medley, Meditation,* and *Butcher's Dance*. The clarinet part is advanced level and is available from draganskimusic.com.

4. *Two Hassidic Dances* for woodwind quintet by Rabbi Michel Twerski, arranged by Edward Benyas, and published by International Opus, contains two upbeat, crowd-pleasing, short movements that were written in 1997. Published by International Opus.

5. *Tants Fraylachs* ("Happy Dance") for clarinet quartet (three B♭ and one bass) by David Warin Solomons is a delightfully well-written piece, perfectly depicting the klezmer style. This is published by Musik Fabrik.

6. *Yerusha* by David Stock. A spirited, eighteen-minute klezmer-style work for solo clarinet, bass clarinet, bassoon, trumpet, trombone, percussion, violin, and double bass. It was commissioned by Michele Zukofsky, Larry Combs, and Richard Stoltzman, and is published by MMB Music Inc.

7. Although Robert Starer's *Kli Zemer* is a concerto for clarinet with band or orchestra, it is also available for clarinet and piano and clarinet with string quartet. This is published by Hal Leonard and available at www.sheetmusicplus .com.

8. Written for this author in 2010 by Romanian composer Serban Nichifor, *Klezmer Dance* is a short, lively trio for violin, clarinet, and piano. A computerized recording and score are available online at free-scores.com/ partitions_telecharger.php?partition=24180.

9. *Hasana Tanz* (E♭, B♭, Bass clarinet) by American composer David Snow is a lively klezmer-influenced wedding dance and was the winning piece on the 1997–1998 Clarinet Trio Composition Contest at Indiana University. Duration is 4'30" And is published by Woodwindiana.

10. *15 Klezmer Solos, Duos, and Trios* is for three clarinets or clarinet/soprano saxophone/trumpet, by Emil Kroitor and Or-Tav Publications. This relatively new book contains a score, parts, and a CD.

QUICK TIP 68: CANDLE 7—KLEZMER RECITAL
REPERTOIRE FOR CLARINET AND LARGE ENSEMBLES

When the opportunity arises to perform as a soloist with large ensembles such as clarinet choir, wind ensemble, band, orchestra, or choral groups, I recommend the following works:

1. *Klezmer Tunes with a Classical Touch* by Daniel Galay contains pieces that are published for clarinet and piano; however, they were also arranged for full clarinet choir by Gregory Barrett (E♭, 3 sopranos, alto, bass, and contra). The composer Daniel Galay arranged them for clarinet and string orchestra. All are published by Or-Tav Publications, and are also available through the Southern Music Company at southernmusic.com/ortav/klezmer.htm.

2. *Klezmer Suite* for clarinet choir and tambourine by Alexis Ciesla is published by Advance Music. In three movements, the *Suite* is based on two traditional klezmer themes and one original composition. It can be played with a drum set and bass (string bass, electric bass, or euphonium). In the absence of a drummer, one of the clarinetists can play the tambourine.

3. *Klezmer Fantasy* for clarinet and wind band by Marcel Saurer has the two-page clarinet part that is moderately difficult and comes with a simple piano score, so it can be performed with piano on a recital as well. It is available at reift.ch and sheetmusic.com.

4. Another work for clarinet with large ensemble is Robert Starer's *Kli Zemer* for either band or orchestra, published by Hal Leonard and available at sheetmusicplus.com. It is a twenty-nine-minute concerto in four movements with klezmer elements. It is also available as a clarinet and piano reduction, as well as clarinet with string quartet.

5. *Torah Orah* (*Yisraeil V'oraita*) is a klezmer-style work for vocal choir and piano with the added bonus of an optional solo clarinet part. It is based on a Hebrew folk song and is arranged by Brant Adams. The clarinet part is almost two pages long and includes a short cadenza. The choir parts are elementary level; however, the solo clarinet part is intermediate level. A piano part and an optional bass part are also included. Published by Santa Barbara Music, this publisher lists several Jewish choral pieces that include clarinet parts. Some are available free of charge at sbmp.com/Instruments.html.

QUICK TIP 69: CANDLE 8—KLEZMER RECITAL REPERTOIRE FOR CLARINET AND STRINGS

Because the fiddle is such a major component in klezmer, it is always gratifying to play the music with ensembles that include strings. Many such works exist, however, some of the sheet music is sometimes challenging to find. The works listed below contain information on how to obtain scores and parts:

1. Probably the best-known classical work with a Jewish influence is Sergei Prokofiev's *Overture on Hebrew Themes, Op. 34* for clarinet, string quartet, and piano. Written in 1919 and published by International Music in 1922, it is considered one of the earliest works to use Jewish ideas from a non-Jewish composer. Prokofiev wrote the piece in one continuous movement during a trip to the United States. The score is very easy to obtain from most music dealers.

2. My favorite work is a trio for violin, clarinet, and piano entitled *The Klezmer's Wedding* by Jewish-Canadian composer Srul Irving Glick. This piece was composed in 1996 and contains a traditional improvisatory opening, followed by a slow dance in three with a fiery ending and can be a real showstopper, especially if played with klezmer techniques and colors. At twelve minutes, it does contain too many repetitions and the ending has a more classical ending compared to folkloric klezmer endings so I would like to refer readers to a modified version played by this author at: youtube.com/ watch?v=ZyIHW73vOLQ. Unfortunately, this piece is increasingly difficult to find. The sheet music may be available at the Canadian Music Centre (CMC) in Toronto or by visiting the composer's website at srulirvingglick. com. Glick also wrote *Suite Hébraïque no. 2* for clarinet, violin, viola, cello, and piano in 1969. The duration is nineteen minutes and it is published by the CMC. Additionally, Glick wrote *Old Toronto Klezmer Suite for Violin, Viola (or clarinet), Cello, Bass, and Piano* in 1998 (seventeen minutes).

3. One of the most ambitious, well-written, and often-played klezmer inspired concert work is *The Dreams and Prayers of Isaac the Blind* for clarinet and string quartet by Argentinian-born Osvaldo Golijob (he later studied composition with George Crumb and joined university faculties in the United States). Thirty-three minutes in duration, it was written in 1994 and published by Ytalianna Music (affiliated with BMI). A version with clarinet and string orchestra is available through Boosey & Hawkes. This work is extremely demanding for the entire group but most especially for the clarinetist who doubles on B♭, A, C soprano clarinets, as well as bass clarinet and optional basset horn. The beginning is absolutely breathtaking with haunting chords, followed by a soaring clarinet line, segueing with interspersed, well-known klezmer tunes.

4. As mentioned earlier, Israeli composer Daniel Galay wrote two volumes for clarinet and piano, entitled *Klezmer Tunes with a Classical Touch. Vol. 1* is also available for clarinet or violin solo with string orchestra or string quartet through the Southern Music Company at southernmusic.com/ortav/klezmer.htm. A separate audio CD of this volume called *Klassical Klezmer* was recorded by this author on the MSR Classics label, MSR 1240, msrcd.com.

5. Another very ambitious work is *Trio for Violin, Clarinet and Piano* by American composer Paul Schoenfield. The four movements are each based partly on Eastern European Hassidic melodies, which can be challenging to sort out at first, therefore, this work is best suited for very seasoned musicians and audiences. Written in 1990, its duration is twenty minutes, and it is available through the composer at hutchinsandrea.com.

6. *Hassidic Fantasy for Clarinet, Cello and Piano* by Ukrainian composer Joachim Stutschewsky is a little-known, but wonderful work filled with klezmer melodies and colors. It is available through Or-Tav Publications at ortav.com (specify work number: SKU 13050).

7. *Esquisses Hebraïques, op. 12* (Hebrew Sketches) by Alexander Krein is a luscious three-movement piece lasting ten minutes. Best of all, the parts are available as free downloads at imslp.org/wiki/Esquisses_H%C3%A9bra%C3%AFques,_Op.12_%28Krein,_Aleksandr_Abramovich%29.

8. *Klezmer Music* for clarinet, viola, and piano (1988) by American composer Elissa Brill, is published by Arsis Press. A partial score can be downloaded at desireisland.com/a/arsispress/scores/brillklezmer.pdf.

9. *Klezmer! Awakening* (1989) for clarinet, guitar, and double bass by Howard J. Buss (b. 1951) is available through the composer's website at http://brixtonpublications.com/howard_j_buss-2.html.

10. American composer Adam Levowitz wrote an unpublished assortment of duets for violin and clarinet, including his intricate *Klezmer Variations*. To contact the composer, visit adamlevowitz.com.

11. *Divertimento from Gimpel the Fool* (1982) for clarinet, violin, cello, and piano by David Schiff is a contemporary style piece in four movements that includes some traditional klezmer tunes, making it an unusual blend. The first movement requires an E♭ piccolo clarinet. This is available through the composer at davidschiffmusic.com.

Two very helpful resources are available to learn about klezmer repertoire with strings are:

1. Patricia Pierce Card's doctoral thesis entitled *The Influence of Klezmer on Twentieth-century Solo and Chamber Concert Music for Clarinet* (2002) can be downloaded free of charge from the University of North Texas Digital Library at: digital.library.unt.edu/ark:/67531/metadc3355.

2. A recording by clarinetist Dieter Klöcker and the Vlach Quartet Prague entitled *Esquisses Hébraïques: Clarinet Quintets on Jewish Themes* can be easily found online.

Fil schpas! (Yiddish for "Enjoy!")

QUICK TIP 70: QUICK-ADVICE BULLETIN BOARD—REPERTOIRE

A broad knowledge of repertoire is crucial for success as a well-rounded performer. You can set yourself apart early on by studying an array of musical styles and periods, making sure to encompass numerous instrumental and vocal combinations, whether or not they include clarinet. Here are some suggestions for the study of repertoire:

- Start building a CD or MP3 library of the main clarinet repertoire and listen to each piece repeatedly to gain insight into clarinet literature and performance styles.
- Become familiar with literature outside the clarinet repertoire by listening to concertos featuring flute, oboe, bassoon, and saxophone, as well as all brass, string, percussion, and keyboard instruments.
- Listen to a wide variety of vocal music including solo, choral, and opera repertoire.
- Familiarize yourself with the main orchestral repertoire such as Bach's *Brandenburg* concertos, Bartók's *Concerto for Orchestra*, Beethoven's symphonies, Brahm's *German Requiem*, Bruckner's symphonies, Copland's *Appalachian Spring*, Debussy's *La mer* and *Prélude à l'après-midi d'un Faune*, Gershwin's *Rhapsody in Blue* and *American in Paris,* Handel's *Water Music* and *Messiah*, Holst's *The Planets*, Liszt's *Hungarian Rhapsody No. 2*, Mahler's *Symphonies*, Mozart's symphonies and *Eine Kleine Nachtmusik*, Orff's *Carmina Burana*, Prokofiev's *Peter and the Wolf*, Ravel's *Boléro* and *Daphnis et Chloé*, Rimsky-Korsakov's *Scheherazade* and *Capriccio Espagnol*, Stravinsky's *Rite of Spring*, Tchaikovsky's *Nutcracker Suite*, Vivaldi's *The Four Seasons*, and Verdi's *Requiem*. Be sure to include all periods such as medieval (years 500–1400), Renaissance (1400–1600), baroque (1600–1750), classical (1730–1820), romantic (1815–1910), modern and twentieth century (1900–2000), contemporary (1975 to present), and twenty-first century (2000 to present).
- Aside from a few baroque works, the clarinet is usually not included in early music periods since the instrument first appeared around 1690. However, many baroque arrangements are available for clarinet, so it is important to study this music in order to play it in the correct style. Listening to recordings of the original instrumentation provides excellent perspective.

- Many ensembles perform early music with the period instruments for which it was intended, such as baroque oboe or the Renaissance shawm. Compare recordings that are done with modern or original period instruments and notice the significant difference in style, tone, and phrasing.
- Broaden your musical comfort zone by listening to music written before the baroque period, such as medieval and Renaissance. Medieval composers include de Vitry and Dufay. Renaissance composers are Byrd, de Lassus, de Machaut, Gabrieli, Gervaise, Josquin des Prez, Léonin, Obrecht, Palestrina, Pérotin, Praetorius, and Sweelinck. Baroque composers are Bach, Corelli, Couperin, Frescobaldi, Handel, Leclair, Lully, Monteverdi, Purcell Rameau, Scarlatti, Telemann, and Vivaldi.
- Expand your horizons yet further by listening to modern, contemporary, and avant-garde composers such as Berio, Berg, Boulez, Cage, Crumb, Glass, Ives, Messiaën, Reich, Satie, Schoenberg, Varèse, and Webern.

A number of very comprehensive websites are available for clarinetists seeking to build their music and recording libraries:

- Gary Van Cott Information Services does the clarinet community a great service by providing a gigantic collection of clarinet books, music, recordings, *Orchestral Musician's* CD-ROMs, videos, and play-along CDs. He put together a spectacular and extra easy-to-navigate website packed with images and descriptions of each product. Visit vcisinc.com.
- Annette Luyben has served the clarinet community for decades. Her extensive website specializes in clarinet repertoire, and expands with offering a vast array of musical styles such as klezmer, jazz, and sacred music. Visit luybenmusic.com.
- Opus-Two, opus-two.com/ClarComposers.html, is an online sheet music store that contains a very large amount of clarinet repertoire listed by composers' last names.
- The International Clarinet Association (ICA) hosts an incomparable clarinet research center at the University of Maryland. Only ICA members and individual students, faculty, and staff at the University System of Maryland may borrow from the ICA Research Center Score Collection. The collection contains an unimaginable amount of clarinet pieces, including rare and hard-to-find compositions from all periods. To join the ICA, visit clarinet.org. To browse the collection online, visit lib.umd.edu/PAL/SCPA/icarcinfo.html.

Several printed books listing specialized clarinet repertoire are available in university libraries as well as the ICA Research Center. Examples include:

- *Clarinet Solos de Concours, 1897–1980: An Annotated Bibliography* by Harry R. Gee (Indiana University Press, 1981). The book lists important clarinet works that were commissioned for the Paris Conservatory's annual competitive examinations until 1980. It includes historical notes and lists approximately seventy pieces.
- The Baylor University Libraries in Texas offer an extensive website listing many bibliographies related to clarinet repertoire. Although these kinds of books naturally get outdated as soon as they hit the shelves, they are important and useful research resources. Visit researchguides.baylor.edu/content .php?pid=42908&sid=316289.

CHAPTER 6

Musicians' Health

QUICK TIP 71: AEROBIC FITNESS FOR LUNG CAPACITY

The word "aerobic" means "with air" or "oxygen," so it is not surprising that aerobic activity helps improve lung capacity. One should be able to have a conversation while doing aerobic exercise. If you are out of breath while talking during exercise, chances are that your long tone capacity on the clarinet will be negatively affected. The increased blood circulation that results from exercising leads to healthy respiratory and cardiovascular systems. The strengthening of the core muscles (including abdominal, back, and chest muscles) opens up the chest cavity and helps develop and maintain good posture. Additionally, aerobic exercise is an excellent stress reliever, a terrific sleep aid, and a great means to increase overall stamina and physical shape.

Aerobic exercise includes such endeavors as running, swimming, biking, rapid walking, or almost anything that increases the heart rate. For best results, these activities should be performed at least twice a week.

When your general outlook is geared toward good, healthy living, your clarinet practice habits will also tend to be healthy, whether this means stretching before playing, avoiding repetitive injury, or practicing without tension.

Some additional ways to increase lung capacity are:

- Start the day with breathing exercises. Before getting up, lie flat on the bed and breathe deeply by slowly inhaling as much as you can, holding for a count of three, then exhaling completely. Although we do not always use our total lung capacity while playing, it is important to develop as much capacity as possible to improve tone projection and phrase duration in general.
- Bypass the elevator when possible and choose to take the stairs instead.
- Consider practicing yoga. Yoga is a great way to improve muscle tone and stretching, which in turn enhances breath control and lung capacity.

There are various breathing resistance exercise gadgets on the market; however, I believe it is not necessary to spend long hours working with them. Instead, use your valuable practice time on your instrument by playing long tones, and use the resistance exercisers only to measure your progress on a weekly or monthly basis.

Needless to say, smoking should be out of the question for anyone, especially wind players.

No matter what your physical condition, you should always check with your doctor before embarking on a strenuous exercise regimen such as those designed to increase lung capacity.

QUICK TIP 72: AVOIDING INJURY

Some students develop repetitive strain injuries because they fail to relax their muscles during practice, or because they develop bad posture, or they take too few breaks during practice sessions. These injuries can be very serious and often impair one's ability to practice and perform. Many of these injuries can be prevented with good practice habits.

Only a few years ago topics such as the dangers of repetitive motion were rarely discussed, but now musicians' health issues are covered in a wide variety of books and articles. Studies show that poor practice habits often result in painful nerve pinching, back pain, or muscle and tendon inflammation.

Ways to avoid muscle and tendon injuries are:

- Choose a time of day to practice when you are not tired.
- Warm up and stretch your muscles before practicing.
- Use a neck strap when necessary.
- Verify that your clarinet thumb rest is positioned at an appropriate height for your hand size.
- Practice difficult technical passages only when you are completely warmed up and have practiced for at least fifteen or twenty minutes beforehand.
- Use correct posture and playing position to avoid unnecessary stress to your back, neck, or shoulders. Practice in front of a mirror to help you maintain a proper posture.
- Pay attention to your body and keep reminding yourself to relax your neck, shoulders, arms, and hands while your practice.
- Take short breaks every half hour during practice.
- If you feel pain, immediately stop practicing and take a break. If the pain persists, seek treatment from a doctor, chiropractor, physical therapist, or massage therapist who is aware of or specializes in musicians' physical issues.
- After practicing, warm down by stretching your muscles.
- Avoid overuse on the computer, as it can compound tendonitis problems in the wrists and hands.
- Avoid risking sports injuries, especially near concert dates.
- Use a book bag with wheels instead of carrying a heavy load on your shoulders.
- Do not practice with a wrist brace, as it prevents fingers from moving freely. Playing with a brace can cause injury because the wrist and fingers have to work harder if constricted during practice. Use the brace only when not practicing and if recommended by a doctor.
- Use earplugs when seated in front of loud brass instruments. Eardrum injuries can be a real danger for musicians.

- Try keeping stress at a minimum before practice sessions and concerts.
- Consider studying the Alexander Technique, which is a method used to improve freedom of movement, balance, support, and coordination.
- Read books such as *Muscle Management for Musicians* by Elizabeth Andrews, *Fit as a Fiddle* by William J. Dawson, *Playing (Less) Hurt* by Janet Horvath, *The Musician's Way: A Guide to Practice, Performance and Wellness* by Gerald Klickstein, *You Are Your Instrument* by Julie L. Lieberman, *A Guide to Preventing and Treating Injuries in Instrumentalists* by Richard Norris, and *The Athletic Musician: A Guide to Playing without Pain* by Barbara Paull and Christine Harrison.

QUICK TIP 73: STRETCHING BEFORE PRACTICE

Some clarinetists may develop repetitive strain injuries because they do not pre-pare their muscles to work efficiently before practice. Furthermore, if the clarinet thumb rest's height is not adjusted properly or if the player spends considerable time practicing without breaks, tension may develop in the hands and wrists. Simple stretching exercises done before each practice session are a great way to minimize muscle strain and increase productivity in the practice room.

When trying to relax your muscles before stretching, avoid shaking your hands and arms to get loose unless you are already warmed up. Shaking tight muscles can damage very small fibers in your tendons and muscles. The only "muscle" that can effectively relax your muscles is the brain.

Adding yoga or Pilates to your activities helps you learn to focus on your breath and coordinate every movement with your breathing, as well as to strengthen the core of your body.

It is important to stop stretching at the onset of any kind of pain, as this is the body's warning signal that the soft tissues are being injured. Stretches should be slow, gradual, and paired with breathing, without any kind of bouncing while you stretch. When stretching, it is good to start out easy and at the neck, then move downward to the shoulders, arms, hands, back, and waist.

Make sure to also cool down your muscles after practice. This helps the muscles recover from their work gradually and helps prevent repetitive strain injury. The stretching exercises listed here are only a sample of the possibilities that can be found in an array of books and websites on the subject. Be sure to maintain good posture while performing the following stretches. Each should be repeated several times.

Examples of warm-up and cool-down stretching:

1. neck rolls
2. shoulder rotations
3. bicep curls
4. hand and finger stretches
5. waist rotations
6. overhead arm stretch

Neck Rolls

Slowly turn your head from left to right. Next, lean your head toward your left shoulder, maintaining awareness of the distance from your ear to your shoulder. Repeat to the right side. These two motions can be combined into a 360-degree neck roll.

Shoulder Rotations

Slowly roll your shoulders in a circular motion through the entire range while maintaining awareness of the space between the ears and the shoulders as well as the movement of the shoulder blades.

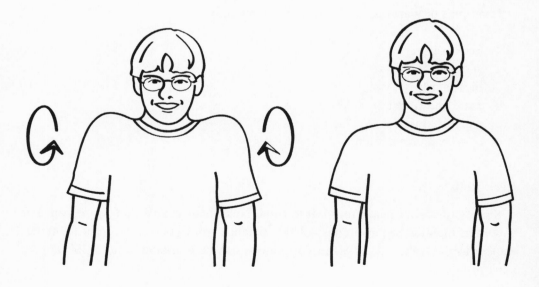

Bicep Curls

Begin with your arms down at your sides. Without moving your elbows, slowly lift your forearms (palms up) until your hands touch your shoulders, then, lower your hands to the original position.

Hand and Finger Stretches

Begin with your elbows at your side and hands held comfortably in front of you. Gently open your fingers away from your palm, extending them as far as can be done comfortably. Then, gently close them into the shape of a fist. Repeat this motion ten times, then try opening and closing each finger, individually.

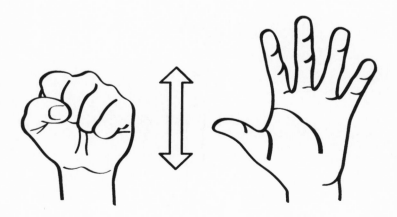

Waist Rotations

Leading with your hands, slowly twist your trunk, both left and right, keeping your head and hips in their original positions by focusing your eyes on an object immediately in front of you. Take deep breaths during this process to increase the stretching effects and promote relaxation.

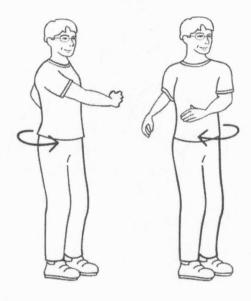

Overhead Arm Stretch

Extend your right hand toward the sky, then reach upward and toward the left until your right arm touches the side of your head. At this point, lift your left arm and grasp your right wrist with your left hand. Gently lean to the left, stretching the right side muscles. Repeat the exercise beginning with the left hand.

QUICK TIP 74: POSTURE—SITTING DOWN

Good posture is very important in the sitting position. It is critical for satisfactory body alignment and allows proper body mechanics while playing. A posture that shows alertness and professionalism sits well with conductors because it demonstrates your attention and readiness to perform under their direction.

Sit with a straight back and open up your torso/leg angle to 45 degrees instead of 90 degrees by lowering one of your legs. This will improve lung capacity and airflow by emulating the standing position. Play with your clarinet at a 35-degree angle and keep the head/neck at a 90-degree angle by looking straight ahead (see illustration below).

One way to help you maintain proper posture in the seated position is to use a specialized chair cushion for musicians to prevent your back from slouching. There are many kinds available online such as contour support cushions or wedge cushions. I don't recommend using the cushion for a long period of time. Instead, use it to make you aware of good posture, then practice without it afterward. This will avoid development of dependency on it or having to carry it to rehearsals and concerts. Learn to play comfortably both in the standing and sitting positions. Both positions need to be exercised in order to strengthen the proper muscles.

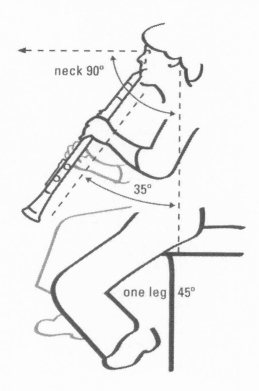

I recommend a book on proper posture for musicians called *The Art of Practicing* by Madeline Bruser and Yehudi Menuhin. The authors describe how to prepare the body and mind to practice with ease as well as how to understand the effect of posture on flexibility and musical expression. A good book not specific to musicians is *The New Rules of Posture: How to Sit, Stand, and Move in the Modern World* by Mary Bond. This is an excellent resource for Pilates, yoga, and dance instructors as well as health care professionals in educating people about postural self-care.

QUICK TIP 75: POSTURE—STANDING UP

Good posture and balance are extremely important for musicians, as they are both necessary to keep the body aligned and allow proper movements and airflow. Playing in an ensemble or simply practicing alone usually involves sitting down. Playing standing up can be more demanding physically, but the perks are many.

When sitting down, the body and legs are usually at a 90-degree angle, slightly compressing the lungs and other internal organs against each other, which in turn can inhibit airflow (see Quick Tip 74: Posture—Sitting Down for details about correct leg angle).

Minimum airflow is not very strenuous and relatively easy to control, but the sound may lack resonance and projection. In a standing position, however, the torso is stretched and the lungs and diaphragm have more freedom to move properly. Standing up allows more airflow, but controlling a larger amount of air may be more demanding and challenging.

Surprisingly, it takes a lot of abdominal and back muscle strength to sit up straight or stand up for an extended period of time. Strengthening your abdominal muscles helps improve posture and balance. Yoga and Pilates instructors offer helpful exercises, such as abdominal crunches using a medicine ball or push-ups, to improve core muscle strength.

A very pleasant and convenient way to practice yoga and strength exercises is using the Wii Fit game by Nintendo. Designed to get video gamers to exercise, it is also a hit with adults who have never even played a video game. Exercises are explained by a virtual trainer and include various fun balance games, sports such as skiing and boxing, and a competitive strength endurance challenge with the trainer.

A unique component is the Wii Balance Board, a plastic surface that connects wirelessly to a Wii console. The yoga and strength-training activities feature a virtual personal trainer that instructs and helps you maintain proper form. Once you stand on the platform, it registers minute shifts in body balance. I suggest standing on the Wii board to test your balance and then playing your clarinet standing on the surface and measure your balance level again.

After improving your balance using the abdominal muscles, you will notice an improvement in how you use your core, abdominal, and lower back muscles, which will improve your breathing. You will also find that your body is centered and anchored more sturdily as you play.

It would be interesting to see how you fare on your first balance test. The Wii Fit registers the degree to which you lean to the right or left and front or back, and it keeps track of your progress each time you use it.

QUICK TIP 76: STAYING HEALTHY—AVOIDING COLDS

Playing a wind instrument is physically demanding, especially with regards to the lungs and embouchure. Musicians cannot afford to be under the weather on the night of a performance. Their reputation is on the line every time they perform, so it is important to maintain a healthy lifestyle and to prevent colds and exhaustion as much as possible.

Cold and flu viruses enter the body through the nostrils, mouth, throat, and eyes. Although it is challenging to avoid contact with viruses throughout the year, some precautions may be taken to minimize the risks.

1. Wash your hands with soap every hour or two, especially during flu season, and use hand sanitizer often.
2. Avoid touching your nose, mouth, and eyes between hand washings.
3. If you feel a cold coming on, immediately gargle with warm salt water or an antiseptic mouthwash such as Listerine.
4. As soon as you feel a tingle in the throat, use an over-the-counter cold preventive medicine such as Zicam (my favorite), Airborne, Cold-EEZE, or zinc lozenges. For best results, treatment should start as early as possible. In my experience, this technique works about 50 percent of the time. I keep the product in my briefcase, desk drawer, and on my nightstand to make sure I have access at critical times. Also, sore throat symptoms often start at night when the body is working overtime to repair itself, and when the immune system might be more vulnerable. Because it is easy to avoid getting up and taking action while in a very sleepy mode, I make sure to have a product on hand at night.
5. At the onset of a sore throat, I suggest doing throat exercises used by singers and yoga practitioners. Vigorously stretch the back of your throat very widely as if yawning or saying "aww" and "ahh," and alternate this movement with stretching the back of the throat the other direction, as if saying "ee" or smiling intensely. This improves blood circulation in this area and can eliminate soreness temporarily or make it disappear if done early on. Repeat as necessary throughout the day, evening, or night.
6. Blowing your nose at least once a day can help reduce viral population.
7. Boost your immune system with foods rich in vitamin C such as citrus fruits, cantaloupe, strawberries, tomatoes, broccoli, cabbage, and red peppers. Vitamin C supplements that contain zinc boost absorption, although the real thing is better than supplements.
8. Drink warm liquids (tea, coffee, hot chocolate), as they prevent viruses from proliferating and wash them from the throat into the stomach where they cannot survive.

9. While in public areas such as schools, avoid directly touching doorknobs, elevator buttons, faucets, or keyboards, and avoid touching your face after contact with these objects.

10. Do not assume that symptom-free individuals are not infected with a cold virus. Symptoms do not show right away and seemingly healthy people who may have already caught a cold can pass it on to others. Needless to say, do not try another person's wind instrument without cleaning it thoroughly beforehand. Similarly, do not share cups or glasses.

11. Drink plenty of water throughout the day. Dehydration weakens the body's ability to fight infection.

12. Eat yogurt with probiotics to help keep the colon healthy, which assists in the effective elimination of viruses and bacteria, and supports a healthy immune system.

13. Decongest your sinuses by turning on the hot water in the shower and slowly breathing in the steam.

14. Sleep with your bedroom window open and door open (if possible) to allow fresh air to circulate. In cold weather months, cracking open the window a fraction of an inch is sufficient. Breathing air in a closed and hermetic room day after day is not recommended, especially if you have a cold or a sinus infection.

15. Get plenty of sleep, exercise, keep fit, and eat healthy foods.

If a cold does surface, these preventive measures can at least lessen the severity and duration of symptoms.

QUICK TIP 77: BRAVING STAGE FRIGHT

Clarinet teachers hear it so many times from students: "But I sounded so much better in the practice room!"

It occurred to me that students prepare their weekly lessons alone in the practice room for *six* days while they perform their lesson in front of a teacher or student group only *one* day each week. Somehow, musicians seem to expect to deliver a perfect performance in front of an audience even though they spent most of their time preparing in a vacant room. Consequently, practicing alone in a cubicle does not adequately prepare us for performing.

Stage fright (or performance anxiety) can arise days, weeks, or even months before the actual event. Some symptoms include a fast pounding heart, shaking hands and legs, dry mouth or excessive salivating, difficulty in swallowing, memory blanks, exaggerated self-consciousness, digestive problems, and nausea. Stage fright can afflict amateur musicians as well as world-acclaimed artists and can vary in severity depending on the concert venue.

Stage fright is a condition that few musicians care to admit, although it is healthy to face the problem and embrace solutions. One may assume that practicing as much as possible before the performance will suffice, but this strategy does not offer any guarantees.

One obvious difference between practicing and performing is that the musician becomes more self-aware when people are present compared to when they are alone. A quick exercise to test this theory would be to see how your concentration is affected if you leave the room door or window open, when more people might hear you practice.

When we practice hour after hour, we enter a zone in which musical concentration is paramount. Our self-awareness seems to disappear and all of our attention is focused on correct fingerings, note attacks, tone nuances, rhythm, and so forth. As soon as additional external factors come into play such as people listening, we suddenly move out of that zone and become much more aware of our bodies and the movements we make. Moreover, some musicians have reported to me that they experience a strange feeling while on stage, suddenly becoming aware of their fingers and bodies to the point that they have a fear of forgetting simple fingerings or even dropping their instruments. Each movement becomes a chore, panic sets in, and the performance is compromised.

The tips that follow will help you to reduce the effects of stage fright and give you the tools to perform at your optimum level.

QUICK TIP 78: CURING STAGE FRIGHT—ENHANCING LIVE PERFORMANCE

Once you have done your preparatory work in the green room and you are about to walk on stage, it is time to transform yourself into a performer who is ready to communicate with a live audience. Here are some concrete solutions to enhance live performance:

1. One idea I find helpful before a casual or semiformal recital is to greet audience members as they enter the recital hall. This makes the experience less formal and gives the performer the impression of performing for friends and acquaintances rather than strangers.
2. Projecting a sense of assertiveness and positive attitude and smiling while entering the stage inevitably makes the audience comfortable and naturally will enhance their overall response. Have you ever noticed how musicians with great bowing skills and stage presence often get thundering applause compared to that received by the sheepish recitalist? Even though a musician may feel stressed or insecure, a display of self-assurance helps alleviate those feelings and if done repeatedly, the feeling of confidence will become a reality.
3. I find that talking to the audience during the performance (between pieces) not only helps to dissipate stress, it is welcomed by listeners. This transforms the event into an interactive experience rather than putting all the weight on the performer's shoulders.
4. Choose appropriate clothing. Planning a concert outfit that makes you feel professional is a great way to build confidence.
5. Naturally, there is the undeniable fact that the more you perform the more you can eventually turn a stressful situation into a simple day-to-day "this is my job" kind of affair.
6. In an ensemble or chamber music situation, it is important to remember that almost everyone in the group is probably feeling some level of performance anxiety, although it might not show. Your peers may worry about mistakes just as much as you do no matter how well they are prepared. The thought of everyone facing the same situation helps put things in perspective.
7. Attend other recitals. Sitting in various recital and concert settings is a good way to put yourself in someone else's shoes. Invariably, you will find that you are mostly concentrating on the music rather than finding each and every flaw in the performance. Realizing this will help you remember that the same is true during your own performance.

QUICK TIP 79: CURING STAGE FRIGHT—PRACTICE STRATEGIES

One key difference between practicing alone and performing live is that practicing alone allows for second chances to repeat difficult passages whereas performing live allows for only one shot. Here are some pointers to follow in the practice room to simulate a live performance:

1. Once you are ready to play through your piece after practicing it thoroughly for several days or weeks, avoid repeating passages during each run-through so that you will have a chance to go through the music as you would during a live performance.
2. Be self-aware as you practice. While practicing, imagine and visualize the concert hall, as well as each person in the audience, the stage spotlights, and the overall ambiance of the evening.
3. Practice random spots in your music and see if you can play them error-free on the first try. This can drastically shift your comfort zone and provide a whole new way to learn challenging sections.
4. Practice with accompaniment as often as possible. This helps you to focus on things other than only your solo part and simulates a live performance situation.
5. Use SmartMusic interactive accompaniment software (visit smartmusic .com). This interactive accompaniment computer program is a fantastic practice and teaching tool. It follows the musician's expressive tempo changes, making it a joy to practice over and over in preparation for rehearsals with a live accompanist later on. It is also a great tool to improve intonation. Most compositions from the main instrumental repertoire are available through an online subscription and new ones can be created using the compatible computer program called *Finale*.
6. Record your practice sessions. Using a recording device allows the performer to be more accountable for what is being practiced if a "tape is rolling." Since we can be our toughest critics, it is essential to listen to and assess each audio clip. An interesting exercise is to turn on the recording device, leave the room, and reenter as if a listener is waiting for us in the practice room.
7. Videotape yourself. Recording both audio and video components of our practice increases our level of self-awareness and therefore helps us simulate a live performance setting.
8. Look in a mirror while you practice. The distraction of seeing yourself playing inevitably will create a distraction similar to that experienced during a live performance.

9. Solfège your entire piece instead of playing it. Also practice your piece using rhythmic solfège instead of traditional solfège. Rhythmic solfège is a helpful sight-reading technique taught in French conservatories. Unlike traditional solfège where the notes are sung with their respective pitch names, rhythmic solfège involves naming each note in rhythm while hand-tapping each beat without singing. Use whichever nomenclature you prefer ("do-re-mi" or "A-B-C"), and start with a slow and steady tempo. Name each note correctly without changing the tempo (naming accidentals is not necessary). This exercise is surprisingly tricky. Start very slowly to avoid stumbling; this enables you to virtually x-ray the music and identify each note more effectively. After some practice, challenge yourself and try the exercise with another person in unison. Using both solfège techniques will expand your knowledge and understanding of the piece and also help with its memorization.

10. Memorize your piece. Even though you may decide to perform with your music as a safety net, memorization can give you an array of backup tools in moments of stress.

11. Rotate and prepare a series of reeds. Needless to say, knowing that you are using a reliable and resonant reed will inevitably reduce your stress level on the concert days.

12. Listening to your most successful past performances is a terrific way to build confidence and to gather clues about what you do best as a musician. It is also a good way to assess shortcomings; however, this exercise is meant to highlight your best qualities to fuel your next performance.

13. Save your lip. It is important not to practice to the point of tiring your embouchure immediately before a scheduled performance. Pace your practice so that you will not experience fatigue or pain in your lip on the day of the concert.

14. Understanding the musical content of a composition allows us to concentrate on the work rather than our own selves during the performance. When our sense of self becomes less important, it allows the musical message to shine through. Understanding the compositional intricacies of a work makes us look forward to conveying a message to the audience, therefore alleviating stress and performance anxiety.

QUICK TIP 80: CURING STAGE FRIGHT—THE BIG PICTURE

It is important to remember that although performance anxiety may feel like an enormous problem at times, it is still quite small compared to the grand scheme of things and that there are issues much "bigger than ourselves" in this world. Here are some insights to consider when performing live:

1. During our musical training years, we are still working on perfecting our art and theoretically, our performance skills improve year by year. Since our skills are less advanced in earlier years, it is possible that the sense of imperfection we felt as younger musicians is inadvertently carried over as we mature. Consequently, the feelings of inadequacy and technical deficiency we experienced in the formative years are deeply imbedded in our memory and can remain unchanged even after we attain professional status as musicians. For example, if we work on a sonata by Brahms at the age of sixteen, the challenging sections of the piece will take several months to master. However, at the age of twenty-one a similarly challenging sonata by Poulenc would only take a few weeks or days to master. But if we decide to perform that same sonata by Brahms again at age twenty-one, the past experience from age sixteen could resurface and give us the feeling of inadequacy even though we now possess more efficient practicing tools. It is important to let go of this train of thought to ensure more peace of mind as performers.
2. Choose a perspective. Perspective can alter our way of thinking in a flash. Imagine you are on your way to play an important solo recital out of town and during the trip you have a car accident that leaves you stranded far from your concert location. Suddenly, the dreadful thought of missing the event makes you wish you were back in your car and racing to your concert. Wouldn't it make sense to adopt this way of thinking without an accident having to take place? I like to think about how lucky I am to be invited to play a concert and how unfortunate it would be to miss the opportunity. This perspective, along with a general sense of positive attitude, can be a wonderful remedy for stage fright.
3. View performing as a way to share artistic ideas rather than being criticized for them.
4. Inspire someone. While performing, one never knows who might be sitting in the audience and be inspired from your musical message. Focusing on what the music can bring into people's lives is yet another way to help shift the focus away from one's self and toward other people.
5. Dedicate your work. Dedicating our performance as a gift to someone who matters can add meaning and purpose to our art and helps us focus on the music rather than ourselves.

6. Performing and sharing a musical message with an audience is the most important reason we study, analyze, practice, and perfect a piece of music. The concert hour is the ultimate moment in a musician's life, and viewed in this way, it can indeed put things into perspective and bring back the joy in performing.

7. Read about performance anxiety. Several books were written on stage fright. Two easy and straightforward reads include *Performance Success: Performing Your Best under Pressure* by Don Greene and *Keeping Your Nerve! Confidence Boosting Strategies for the Performer* by British author Kate Jones.

Affiliated with the Juilliard School of Music in New York City, sports psychologist Don Greene teaches seven main skills to prepare musicians to perform at the highest possible level, including determination, poise, mental outlook, emotional approach, attention, concentration, and resilience.

Keeping Your Nerve! is a pocket-sized guide offering advice to help conquer the fear of performing in public and ultimately becoming comfortable on stage.

QUICK TIP 81: QUICK-ADVICE BULLETIN BOARD—MUSICIANS' HEALTH

The first wealth is health. — Ralph Waldo Emerson, American poet

Here are some preventive tips regarding musicians' health:

Body

- Make time for physical activity. The benefits of exercise are obvious and the discipline required for physical activity will carry over in the practice room, and vice versa.
- Keep headphones' or earbuds' volume low to save your hearing.
- Avoid abiding by the old saying: *No pain, no gain.* Listen to your body, learn to play without tension, and temporarily suspend practice if pain sets in. If any pain persists, consult a physician or chiropractor with experience in treating musicians.
- Read *Playing (Less) Hurt: An Injury Prevention Guide for Musicians* by Janet Horvath. It is a detailed guide for a healthy approach to music making and is very well written. It includes many lists such as warm-up stretches, injury danger signals, musician's travel survival kit, helpful suggestions for teachers, hearing protection tips, detailed practice schedules, proper equipment, and advice to conductors. A website related to the book is playinglesshurt .com.
- Need it be spelled out to wind instrumentalists? Do not smoke and stay far away from secondary smoke.

Mind

- Exercise, both physical and mental, is important. It increases blood flow and gets oxygen to your brain. The brain, like a muscle, gets stronger with use. To keep your mind sharp, engage in intellectual challenges, such as sight-reading contemporary etudes like *Preliminary Exercises and Etudes in Contemporary Techniques for Clarinet* by Ronald L. Caravan, and *16 Modern Etudes* for *Clarinet, Op.14* by Frantisek Zitek.
- Learn to alleviate stress by reading books such as the *Don't Sweat the Small Stuff* series by Richard Carlson. I occasionally recommend these books to

skeptical students who inevitably come back pleasantly surprised after reading his eye-opening tips.

- If you feel stressed every day, look for ways to eliminate extra activities in your week so you will have more time to devote to the most important things in your life.
- Stress-reducing techniques include yoga, meditation, hot baths, relaxing music, and breathing exercises. The idea of breathing exercises may sound clichéd, but they work like magic because oxygen is a great mood enhancer. Wind players manage air every day; however, they might forget to truly *breathe*. Take a slow, deep breath, hold it in for a few seconds, exhale, and notice how your mood improves instantly.

Nutrition

Read *Food Rules: An Eater's Manual* by Michael Pollan. It is a fun and quick guide filled with sound nutrition advice like "Don't eat anything your great-grandmother wouldn't recognize as food," "Eat mostly plants," "Shop the peripheries of the supermarket and stay out of the middle," and "Avoid foods you see advertised on television."

- Drink plenty of water every day, especially in the twenty-four-hour period prior to a big performance, to help prevent dry mouth caused by performance anxiety.
- Avoid drinking coffee or ingesting caffeine before concerts, as it will result in increased stress levels.
- Limit intake of fast food and soft drinks. They only look like food and contain very few nutrients and fail to fuel hard-working bodies and minds properly.
- Develop the habit of always eating breakfast. Consider choosing high-fiber foods, fruit, or probiotic yogurt that helps promote better vitamin absorption, improves digestion, and fortifies the immune system.
- Eat only when you are hungry, with the exception of breakfast as suggested previously.
- Avoid carbohydrates immediately before practicing, especially those highly caloric and sugary pastries and candy bars. Your energy level might increase temporarily but then decrease once the "sugar high" disappears.
- Become the type of person who would take vitamins, but doesn't need to because of healthy eating habits.
- Buy smaller plates and eat smaller portions. It takes about twenty minutes for a meal to fill the stomach, so stop eating before you are full and you will feel satisfied within twenty minutes.

- Eat foods that are known as "superfoods" because of their antioxidant, immune-system-boosting properties. These include whole grains and brightly colored fruits and vegetables like berries, cantaloupe, red grapes, mangoes, nectarines, peaches, tomatoes, asparagus, beets, broccoli, Brussels sprouts, carrots, collard greens, kale, spinach, sweet potatoes, and turnip. Detailed information on superfoods can easily be found online and in nutritional books and articles.

Sleep

- Get enough sleep every night. Most importantly, do not wait to until you are completely exhausted or feeling dizzy before going to sleep, as this may wear you down and negatively impact your health over time.
- Be aware that sleeping patterns can be disrupted during concert tours because of the long travel hours, different sleeping environments in hotels, late nights, and changing time zones.
- Problems related to sleep could be an indicator of other problems and may warrant the attention of a physician.

CHAPTER 7

Music Profession

QUICK TIP 82: CONCERT ATTIRE

Dress poorly, and people will notice your clothes; dress well, and people will notice you. —Coco Chanel, French fashion designer

Wearing a high-quality concert outfit will make you look sharp and professional, and enhance your confidence. Additionally, it shows your commitment and respect for your art, your ensemble, and your audience. Some basic rules are:

1. Keep your clothes clean and simple.
2. Clothing size does not matter. Perfect fit matters.
3. Choose clothes that combine classic style with current fashions.
4. Maintain your concert wardrobe with regularly cleaning and pressing.
5. Keep your shoes clean and polished.
6. Body grooming is equally important.
7. Avoid strong fragrances on the concert stage.
8. Show good taste.
9. Find your look. Ask for feedback from friends and family.
10. Abide by the required orchestra or ensemble concert dress codes.

Professional concert dress code examples for symphony orchestras are:

Concert Black (women): long formal black dress (at least ankle length and moderate neckline), or black skirt, or black formal dress slacks. Black or white formal blouse (all sleeve lengths are acceptable, however thin shoulder straps should be covered with a jacket or dressy cardigan). Dark or neutral hose, black dress shoes. Accessorize conservatively and formally, and use soundless jewelry and unscented body products.

Concert Black (men): black tuxedo, white dress shirt, black bow tie, black vest or cummerbund, black socks, black dress shoes. Use unscented body products.

Exceptions occur for informal or outdoor concerts and are usually designated as White, or Black and White.

Dress codes vary depending on settings such as jazz ensemble, marching band, concert band, choir, chamber music groups, or solo recitals.

If you have trouble deciding on what to wear for ensemble concerts, it is always better to be overdressed than underdressed. Make it a priority to look sharp, distinguished, clean cut, and professional.

QUICK TIP 83: STAGE PRESENCE AND ETIQUETTE

Stage Presence

Singers and actors develop their stage presence skills early on in their education. They are taught to treat their lessons as mini-performances, so they arrive well dressed, display their best and most professional behavior, and are ready to perform each week's assignment as if it were a public performance. Unfortunately, few instrumentalists focus on these skills as part of their education, yet they have every bit as much potential to appeal to their audience as soon as they walk on stage.

Audience members attend concerts in hopes of seeing a good show and they want to believe that you are just as happy to be standing on stage as they are to be sitting in the audience. No matter how anxious you might feel, make sure to enter the stage smiling and showing your audience how much you appreciate them being there for you.

Before bowing, look straight out into the audience with a sparkle in your eyes, wait two seconds, and gently bow with your feet together. If you are playing a solo recital with piano accompaniment, remember to acknowledge your accompanist before the recital starts and after each piece. When counting rests, be sure to remain engaged with the music and respect the accompanist's musical moment.

There are many performance setting possibilities (solo recital with or without accompaniment, solo with orchestra, chamber music) and helpful suggestions are discussed for each one in excellent books such as *Beyond Talent: Creating a Successful Career in Music* by Angela Myles Beeching and *Stage Presence from Head to Toe: A Manual for Musicians* by Karen A. Hagberg.

Stage Etiquette

If you need a glass of water on stage, it is important to place it on some surface other than the piano. There are good reasons that pianists and piano technicians often remind us not to treat a piano as a piece of furniture. Placing a glass of water (or any other object) on a piano is not only poor etiquette, it can also damage the piano finish, not to mention that it can accidentally spill on the inside of the instrument.

Avoid playing an encore unless the audience is calling out for more with continuous applause and loud bravos. Performances are usually designed to end with a showy piece, so playing an encore, no matter how great it is, can sometimes be anticlimactic.

If you need time to reenter the stage with a group of musicians, refrain from bowing if the applause ends while members of the group are still walking on stage.

Above all else, do not return to the stage for a second bow unless it is warranted by a healthy dose of applause. Performances that earn return bows are a source of inspiration for musicians. However, returns to the stage should be reserved for only those occasions on which the audience responds with exceptional enthusiasm.

QUICK TIP 84: WHAT NOT TO DO ON STAGE

You've practiced for hours to perfect your music. Now it's time to play in public, either at a rehearsal or concert. Here are a few suggestions that can help you make the most positive overall impression on those who hear you:

- When entering the stage, make sure to bow while the applause is still going on. If it stops before you are center stage, skip bowing.
- When bowing, keep your feet close together to enhance a professional stance. Bowing with feet far apart looks awkward and inelegant.
- Avoid extended efforts to tune your instrument on stage. A quick tuning will suffice, especially if you did the correct tuning preparation beforehand.
- Avoid practicing your ensemble solos loudly when you warm up on stage in front of the audience. This diminishes the effect of your actual performance and may be considered less than gracious in the eyes of your peers.
- If you need water on stage, use an attractive, real, non-plastic drinking glass instead of a water bottle if possible.
- If you need to swab your instrument between movements during a solo recital where you are the main person on stage, avoid swabbing repeatedly, as a good swab will do the job with one swipe.
- When you have a water buildup in a tone hole, clear the moisture as quietly as possible. This will be welcomed by the conductor, your peers, and your audience.
- Avoid frowning when you make a mistake during a performance. This will emphasize the error and detract from the overall effect.
- Avoid playing in a shy manner. Project your sound and play confidently. Audiences respond more positively to assertive performers, whether or not mistakes occur.
- If sitting in an ensemble facing the audience, avoid wearing clothing that is too short or does not cover the legs sufficiently. Your outfit might look great when you try it on standing up in front of a mirror; however, the look may be ruined in the seated position.
- Avoid playing loudly in the green room near the stage door while your colleagues are performing. Waiting for your turn shows courtesy and respect toward your peers, and prevents the audience from unwillingly hearing two performers at once.
- When deciding on lighting in a small recital hall, remember to turn off the house lights before going on stage so that the ambiance is as planned and the audience does not have blinding lights shining at them.

- When you play in a dark pit for operas, ballets, or musicals, make sure your stand light does not shine directly toward the audience.

Sometimes the smallest details are the ones that make the biggest difference and result in a performance that is as perfect and smooth as can be. In music, the silence during rests often has a greater musical impact than the notes we play. Likewise, the things we don't do are as important as the things we do.

QUICK TIP 85: WHAT TO DO OFF STAGE

If you can't say anything nice, then don't say anything at all. — Aesop, writer (c. 620–560 BC)

One of the most important factors in our success is how well we interact with others. Whether teaching or being taught, we spend a significant amount of time in the clarinet studio. Constructive criticism is necessary in this setting, so it is not surprising that many of us tend to be harsh critics, but we must be careful of what we do and say inside and outside of the studio.

Here are some other suggestions that will help you to get the most of your professional relationships:

- Avoid being overly critical of others' efforts. This applies not only to one's playing abilities, but also to their choice of equipment, program music, musical interpretation, and so on. This is not to say that you should send out a constant stream of superlatives, as doing so may damage your credibility in the long run.
- Answer messages and phone calls cordially and promptly.
- Be a good listener. People know when you are preoccupied with other thoughts while conversing.
- If you must decline a performance request, be helpful by suggesting a highly qualified replacement if possible.
- If you are hiring other musicians for a performance, avoid embarrassing them by making them ask how much the job pays. The amount of compensation, or lack thereof, should be one of the first things you discuss.
- Be willing to help others. Carry equipment, help set up the stage, or offer to turn pages for piano accompanists.
- When in need, ask others for assistance. While we may find it noble to avoid imposing on others, asking for their help often strengthens bonds and professional relationships.
- Attend others' concerts. You know how much you appreciate it when your peers attend your events. Return the favor when possible.
- Smile and be positive. People like to associate with those who are uplifting.
- Be dependable and do what you say you will do. Show up on time. Be sure to enter any commitments into your calendar immediately upon acceptance. Failure to do so can result in missed obligations and a loss of confidence in your dependability as a professional.
- Manage your time efficiently. Respect deadlines and submit completed assignments ahead of time. Avoid doing things too hurriedly or at the last minute.

- Follow procedure. When receiving assignments, read the fine print to avoid misunderstandings.
- Stay clear of politics. Remain cordial at all times, no matter what. Stop conflicts before they start and own up to your mistakes.
- Have a neat office, practice room, or classroom. Eliminate out-of-date papers and get rid of the clutter on a daily basis. The appearance of your work environment says a lot about your work habits and is more inviting to visitors, not to mention that an organized environment facilitates more efficient use of time.

QUICK TIP 86: READING BUSINESS BOOKS

At some point, when you finally land your dream job as a performer or music educator, one of your priorities will be to keep your job for years to come. Although popular belief says that being a great musician is sufficient to remain employed, I believe that work ethic is one of the most important elements necessary for lasting success as a musician, especially when the job market is tight.

Musicians often see themselves as anything but employees and might prefer to concentrate on the artistic and creative side of their positions and put aside the business aspects of their career-building endeavors. Musicians should be savvy and know how to increase their value as either employees or self-employed persons. One way to learn more about this topic is to borrow ideas from the corporate world. Those with careers in business receive a steady stream of self-improvement information beginning with college courses and continuing with professional development training by their employers. Fortunately for us, musicians have access to myriad books that were written primarily with businesspeople in mind.

Some principles of work ethics are common sense but they are not often studied in depth in music schools. I suggest reading some of the self-improvement books aimed at business people to help gather the psychological tools needed to implement solid job-retention strategies.

Self-improvement Books

Don't Sweat the Small Stuff—and It's All Small Stuff by Richard Carlson. I find this book to be a perfect first step to develop optimism in general and ultimately help promote positive attitude and good work ethic. The text is extremely easy to read and describes many ways to reduce stress by modifying one's perspective on problems. The tips are fun to read, and the book's small size makes it easy to bring anywhere. Personally, it has helped me on many levels and consequently, I recommend it to all my students on a yearly basis.

Another book in Dr. Carlson's *Don't Sweat the Small Stuff* series is called *Don't Sweat the Small Stuff at Work: Simple Ways to Minimize Stress and Conflict While Bringing Out the Best in Yourself and Others.* This book provides priceless advice for the workplace. It teaches ways to modify the things we can control like our own outlook and behavior. Some of the principles illustrated in the book may seem obvious; however, they become more realistic and easier to apply when we see them in black and white.

Vision and Flexibility

I believe that two of the most important qualities to have in today's job market are vision and the flexibility to adapt to change. I found a most unusual and helpful book that addresses this in less than one hundred pages: *Who Moved My Cheese? An Amazing Way to Deal with Change in Your Work and in Your Life* by Spencer Johnson and Kenneth Blanchard. Although at first, one may think the presentation of subject matter is simplistic (the font is very large, and the book includes drawings, resembling a children's storybook), a closer look will reveal that it contains an amazingly clever story filled with wise advice and witty plays on words. The book illustrates how change can be viewed either as a blessing or a curse, depending on one's perspective. The story is about modifying attitudes toward change in life, especially at work, and advocates how to anticipate change, let go of the old, and predict the new.

Time Management

An important skill to put into practice in the workplace is time management. For some, this may seem to be self-evident, yet others find themselves wishing for more hours in the day to accomplish everything that needs to be done. I found a wonderfully practical little book on this topic entitled *Improve Your Time Management* by Polly Bird. She offers strategies for planning, conquering procrastination, learning to delegate, reducing paperwork and phone time, dealing with information overload, using a daily planner, and making time for fun activities. A very easy read, it tackles issues in an efficient way, which is the core of this book.

Creativity

The latest studies indicate that one of the very top qualities required at work is creativity (good examples are companies like Apple and Google). In his fascinating book, *A Whole New Mind—Why Right-Brainers Will Rule the Future*, author Daniel H. Pink offers a brilliant essay on how the virtues of right-brain thinking can increase chances for high-quality employability in the future, and how the "MFA is the new MBA" (master of fine arts/master of business administration). He describes how artistic and intuitive individuals will become leaders in the ongoing Conceptual Age, as opposed to left-brain thinking that was imperative in the Information Age. This book is a must for musicians.

Becoming Indispensable in the Workplace

One of the best ways to increase job security is to enhance our value, whether it be through our excellent work ethic, productivity, or creativity. These qualities can tip the scale in our favor during cutbacks in the workplace. There are many wonderful books offering invaluable insights on this topic. Some classic titles are:

- *The Indispensable Employee*, by Eric Weber, is a short and to-the-point little treasure of a book.
- *Becoming an Indispensable Employee in a Disposable World,* by Neal Whitten, describes ways that employees should "earn their jobs every day."
- *How to Be the Employee Your Company Can't Live Without: 18 Ways to Become Indispensable*, by Glenn Shepard, offers insight from the perspective of the employer and on how workers can increase their prospects for raises and promotions.
- *How to Be a Star at Work—9 Breakthrough Strategies You Need to Succeed*, by Robert E. Kelley, shows how the author studied the differences between superior workplace performers and their average peers and determined that such stars are made, not born. He describes his well-known tactics, including initiative, networking, self-management, leadership, teamwork, and organizational savvy, among others.
- *169 Ways to Score Points with Your Boss*, by Alan R. Schonberg, Robert L. Shook, and Donna Estreicher, has the perspective that employers can help workers acquire skills that can improve marketability down the line. The 169 insightful tips are short and to the point and can be read in any order.
- *How to Win Friends and Influence People*, by Dale Carnegie, must be included in any discussion about how to flourish in the workplace. This is the original self-help book, and while it was first published in 1937, it remains relevant today.

More recent titles are:

- *101 Ways to Stand Out at Work*, by Arthur D. Rosenberg, is a wonderful book that offers practical advice on how to become more engaged and rise to the top at work. The 101 titles are cleverly phrased, such as "Intelligence is learning from your own mistakes," "Wisdom is learning from the mistakes of others," "Turning down an assignment can turn off the boss," and "Networking pays off your investment with interest."
- *5 Steps to Professional Presence*, by Susan Bixler and Lisa Scherrer Dugan, has a format that is a little like a textbook and includes candid advice on improving interpersonal relationships, how to dress at work, cell phone etiquette, resolving conflicts diplomatically, turning negatives into positives, social savvy, as well as business etiquette in and out of the workplace.
- *The 10 Laws of Enduring Success*, by Maria Bartiromo, describes ten personal qualities that lead to success, such as self-knowledge, vision, initiative, courage, integrity, and resilience. She offers unapologetic advice such as "Control your fate, or someone else will," "Be bold, smart, and fair," "Write your epitaph every day," and "Fight for yourself."

- *Nice Girls Don't Get the Corner Office 101: Unconscious Mistakes Women Make That Sabotage Their Careers*, by Lois P. Frankel, is targeted at a specific audience; however, it can be helpful for everyone. The author explains why some workers forge ahead in their careers while others stay behind. She describes 101 behaviors that are learned in childhood that can sabotage careers later on, and offers coaching tips to alleviate them and develop thriving careers. Some mistakes she lists are Working without a Break, Tolerating Inappropriate Behavior, Limiting Your Possibilities, and Ignoring the Importance of Network Relationships.

Tenure

A note to musicians who will eventually work toward earning tenure as orchestra musicians or educators: I believe that earning tenure (or permanent status) is best regarded as the start of a great thing rather than the end of a challenge. A person could choose to regard the tenure process as a series of "hoops to jump through"; however, a person with a positive attitude and solid work ethic prefers to see tenure as a valuable box of tools that is designed to help learn the job and propel their career forward. Tenured musicians will have learned to use these tools so well that they cannot help but continue to utilize them and honor their discipline by becoming invaluable members of the profession.

QUICK TIP 87: PROFESSIONALISM AND WORK ETHIC

As mentioned in Quick Tip 86: Reading Business Books, getting a job is one thing, keeping it is another. I propose combining artistry and corporate savvy to increase job retention power. After all, we invest years of practice in order to achieve our artistic goals. Why not apply this practice discipline to achieve greater success with our career development as well? While extraordinary musical skill is paramount to winning an audition or teaching position, integrity, work ethic, positive attitude, and foresight will seal the deal down the road and increase our value as employed persons.

Countless online business surveys report that beyond skill and knowledge, employers consider work ethic and attitude as critical factors during the interviewing process. Even the most talented musicians can jeopardize employment success by failing to display these qualities. Good work ethic translates into being personally accountable and responsible for our work. Four important qualities include interpersonal skills, creativity, initiative, and dependability.

Artists depend on audiences to receive and acknowledge their work, and interpersonal skills are vital to the success of this exchange. Having professional connections can make a vast difference in a musical career but more importantly, the impression we make when interacting with our colleagues or mentors can make the real difference down the line and significantly improve the quality of these connections.

Creativity is a quality that artists must possess in a world where financial profit is prevalent and can often eclipse the value of some artistic ventures.

Initiative is a very important characteristic for artists. Today's workplace is characterized by more freedom and less direct supervision. For example, clarinet professors are hired at universities with the understanding that their studios should grow and function successfully, and that students will thrive at the institution. Although professors might not be specifically advised on how to achieve this, it is understood that it should happen, one way or another. Lack of initiative or vision, procrastination, and missed opportunities can jeopardize the professor's success.

Being dependable is one of the most highly sought after traits in and out of the workplace. This includes honesty, reliability, and being on time. Lack of dependability can result in the loss of credibility with colleagues and students. Other important qualities in the workplace are:

- Attendance: arriving on time and giving advance notice of absence, as well as sending a substitute in performance or classroom situations.
- Character: loyalty, honesty, trustworthiness, initiative, positive attitude, self-discipline, healthy self-confidence, responsibility, patience, and maintaining appropriate relationships with superiors, peers, and students.

- Teamwork: respecting the rights of others, good communication and leadership skills, and cooperation.
- Appearance: appropriate appearance and etiquette.
- Productivity: being ready to deliver high-quality assignments on time, perform repertoire or teach lessons according to plan, and create innovative ways to disseminate our art.
- Organizational skills: skills in time management, stress management, paperwork, prioritizing, flexibility, and a clean office, practice room, classroom or studio.

Thought for the Day

Although I am offering musicians ways to borrow ideas from the corporate world to improve employability, I also want to invite corporate persons who have not yet done so to join in our artistic world and borrow ideas from musicians and artists to improve their creativity and outlook in the workplace as well. By trading strategies, we can learn to accomplish different things in a multitude of positive ways.

QUICK TIP 88: QUICK-ADVICE BULLETIN BOARD—MUSIC PROFESSION

Without music life would be a mistake. —Friedrich Wilhelm Nietzsche, German philosopher

• Realize that the student/teacher relationship is a two-way street and that teachers will give a mile if you give an inch. Accept some responsibility for motivating your teacher to give you everything they have to offer by being interested, well-prepared, proactive, and armed with well-thought-out questions. These factors go hand in hand and support each other. For example, when the student comes to a lesson well-prepared, the teacher is excited and inspired to coach at a higher level. The student, in turn, absorbs this newly learned material and is able to ask about specific issues and receives insightful answers to these problems. The lessons become customized and the teacher naturally wants to go the extra mile. Lessons turn into teamwork because both parties are doing their share.

• During rehearsals, show conductors your professionalism by sitting up straight and paying close attention to their instructions while they address the ensemble. Above all, resist infamous habits such as reading, talking, or texting while sitting through countless rests or *tacet* movements during long rehearsals. Use those moments to study and mark your part or learn conducting and rehearsal techniques from the director's comments to the rest of the ensemble. This will help you understand the music in greater depth. Furthermore, bring water instead of hot beverages to rehearsals, as the latter's aroma may distract colleagues and could result in a messy and embarrassing spill.

• Read *Becoming an Orchestral Musician: A Guide for Aspiring Professionals*, by British author Richard Davis. This is an important addition to the literature because very few books on orchestral playing zoom in on the performer's perspective. It includes sound advice related to orchestral auditions, how to cope with nerves, ins and outs of ensemble versus solo playing, conductors, and how orchestras and other ensembles function. The book includes interesting quotes and anecdotes taken from several interviews conducted with BBC Philharmonic musicians, as well as other soloists, chamber musicians, educators, music critics, and managers.

• Read Dave Atkins' article entitled *Tips for Freelancers* included in a small book called *Clarinet Masterclasses*, published by Windplayer. Atkins discusses the pros and cons of freelance work, offers tips on how to practice for studio gigs, and describes personal qualities necessary to be successful as a studio musician. The book includes fifteen short articles written by well-known clarinetists who discuss topics ranging from reed work, breathing technique, phrasing, tone, intonation, and articulation.

CHAPTER 8

Extra Tips

QUICK TIP 89: COLLEGE MUSIC AUDITIONS—PREPARATION

Preparing for college auditions requires good planning skills, hard work, and perseverance. Applicants who plan on majoring in music need the support of parents, teachers, and friends to be successful. Competition is fierce so it is crucial to follow important steps beforehand.

1. Start practicing well in advance and take lessons from a trusted teacher for at least two years before your audition. Choose music that will best show off your strengths and select repertoire that appears repeatedly on your prospective colleges' lists so you will not be overwhelmed by learning too many pieces. Study professional recordings of this repertoire.
2. Focus on good fundamentals. Teachers usually prefer students with a solid foundation who do not need to relearn basic techniques. Remember to practice scales, arpeggios, and sight-reading.
3. Rhythm is critical in sight-reading, so focus on playing without stopping, and remember to always read the key signature before starting.
4. Purchase a professional-model clarinet early on, if possible. Auditioning on a professional instrument often yields better results even if the instrument is borrowed. Make sure your instrument is in perfect working order several weeks before starting college. If you do not have a high-end instrument a few months before your audition, wait to select one with advice from your new teacher during your first semester in college.
5. Perform mock auditions for your teacher, ensemble director, friends, and family.
6. Participate in honor, region, and state auditions, and perform with high-level groups as much as possible.

7. Give ample notice to people writing your recommendation letters and provide them with preaddressed, stamped envelopes when required. If applicable, check the agreement box not to have access to each letter, as this will add to the credibility of the recommendation.

8. Arrive early for auditions as schedules often change at the last minute due to cancellations. Dress appropriately, demonstrate professionalism at all times, and address faculty using proper etiquette during the entire process.

9. Be flexible when asked to play a section in a different manner.

10. If a piano accompaniment is required, plan sufficient rehearsal time before your audition. If the school offers the option of providing a same-day accompanist, choose to play unaccompanied so you will not be distracted by unexpected musical variance.

11. Ask if you can chat with one or two clarinet studio members during your audition or visit.

12. A few days after your auditions are completed, send handwritten thank-you letters to the instructors who met with you, whether or not you plan on attending their schools.

QUICK TIP 90: COLLEGE MUSIC AUDITIONS—CHOOSING A SCHOOL

Before choosing a school, it is important to focus on personal fit and to make sure to visit several colleges in person in order to increase option outcomes. Here are some steps to facilitate your search:

1. Discuss the reputation of various schools with your teacher and with enrolled students. However, avoid choosing a school simply because it is famous. Evaluate schools in accordance with your performance skills, educational needs, and based upon where you can market yourself competitively to increase your chances of earning scholarships. On the other hand, choosing a school where a teacher will go to bat for you throughout your career may eventually prove to be priceless compared to a full-tuition scholarship.

2. Contact each clarinet professor to schedule a trial lesson approximately one year before your audition. The lessons will be your chance to assess compatibility and teaching styles. Ask about studio size, number of openings, placement record, ensemble opportunities, teaching philosophy, and scholarship prospects. Choose teachers who answer your e-mails, invite you to campus, offer preaudition advice, and follow up after your visits. This will give you an idea how much attention you will receive as a student. Most importantly, choose a teacher whose playing you admire and who will actively help you reach your professional goals. Keep in touch so your name stands out when it is time for scholarship recommendations.

3. Include both conservatory and liberal arts music programs on your list and narrow the number of finalists to between three and five schools. If your list is too long, applied teachers may offer scholarships to other qualified candidates who are more likely to accept them.

4. Applied college faculty can be classified as full-time or adjunct. Depending on the circumstances at a particular college, there is a good chance that an adjunct instructor is a full-time performer. In contrast, full-time college instructors may perform regularly, but teaching is their main responsibility. If it is important to you to study with an individual who is currently involved in full-time performance, an adjunct instructor might be your best choice. However, if you want a teacher who is readily available, a full-time professor would likely be a better fit. Note that in a few cases, individuals are both full-time faculty and performers.

5. Strictly follow application and scholarship requirements shown on the school's website. Some colleges have separate applications for the university and music school.

6. Once you choose a school and are assured of your acceptance, notify the other institutions in case they may be holding a place for you that could go to someone else. Always remember that the music world is very small. How you act now will be noticed and remembered for a long time to come.

QUICK TIP 91: HOW TO BE MORE MARKETABLE

Eighty percent of success is showing up.—Woody Allen, Dixieland jazz clarinetist, comedian, and film director

Becoming a musician is an exciting but challenging career path. Competition is fierce and job opportunities are limited. Making yourself more marketable is a great way to increase your chances of securing employment in the profession. Beyond the obvious pointers such as performing to the highest standards and arriving at engagements on time, important qualities sometimes overlooked by musicians should be developed early on, such as entrepreneurial, marketing, and business skills.

In his book, *Purple Cow: Transform Your Business by Being Remarkable*, best-selling author, entrepreneur, and marketing specialist Seth Godin affirms that the key to success is to find a way to stand out just as a purple cow in a pasture would be eye-catching. Reading books on marketing is a clever way to tap into the "real" world to see how you can stand apart from myriad other musicians. Reading this book helped me develop ideas I would have not imagined beforehand, such as distributing complimentary clarinet studio stickers to incoming college students. The stickers display my website URL and may be seen by other prospective students down the road.

A much more comprehensive book on this subject is *The Savvy Musician*, by David Cutler. Intended specifically for musicians, the 350-page book is packed with priceless advice on how to stand out from the crowd. Cutler covers topics such as career building, earning an income, branding, fund-raising, building an audience, image, networking, budgeting and investing, creating press kits and websites, recordings, copyright and licensing, freelancing, performing strategies, concert etiquette, music technology, interdisciplinary performance, and education. Best of all, it includes 165 fascinating stories about real, proactive musicians who created successful careers for themselves.

One way to strengthen your career path in music is to find a niche that will make you more marketable in a relatively short amount of time. Do you have a special talent or attribute that could accelerate the recognition of your skills? Are you a star player who has a strong knack with technology? Do you have ancestry that you could tie in to enhance your repertoire? Are you fascinated by other arts that could transform your performances into interdisciplinary events? The idea is to find formulas that have not been overly tapped into so that you can attract more diverse audiences and get noticed early on.

Some books targeting musicians and music teachers who wish to increase their marketability include *The Business of Getting More Gigs As a Professional Musician*, by Bob Popyk, and *The PracticeSpot Guide to Promoting Your Teach-*

ing Studio: How to Make Your Phone Ring, Fill Your Schedule, and Create a Waiting List You Can't Jump Over, by Philip Johnston. Both titles offer helpful advice on ways to promote yourself and view performing and teaching as a business.

Additional ways to expand your skills and marketability are to:

- Learn second, E♭, and bass clarinet orchestral parts rather than focusing only on principal parts to increase your audition outcome potential.
- Study jazz, Dixieland, and klezmer.
- Consider auditioning for military bands.
- Hone your teaching skills.
- Acquire skills in arranging.
- Learn how to transpose (this helps tremendously in all kinds of settings such as jazz improvisation, playing other instruments' parts, and orchestral repertoire in C).
- Develop the ability to play by ear.
- Double on instruments such as saxophone, flute, and oboe. This allows you to play musicals, play in jazz bands, and expand your teaching studio.
- Acquire skills in instrument repair.
- Post your own professional website.
- Print some business cards and carry them with you at all times.
- Develop some skills with foreign languages.
- Be outgoing and sociable and work to develop your public speaking skills. These qualities will enhance the effectiveness of your networking as well as your classroom teaching.
- Develop your interviewing skills. Take advantage of one of the many books written for job seekers or enlist the help of a mentor to help you practice with mock interviews.
- Use a smartphone so you will have quick access to business texts or e-mails.

There is a popular belief that in 1899, U.S. Patent Office Commissioner Charles H. Duell said: "Everything that can be invented has been invented." History proved that this statement was premature. New playing styles, tastes in music, and technologies continually bring about new musical possibilities and combinations to be explored. While it may be difficult to imagine that new concepts are still there for us to discover, it is indeed possible to find niches and new ideas to distinguish you from other contenders. Reading materials related to marketing can inspire you to do just that.

QUICK TIP 92: FINANCIAL PLANNING FOR MUSICIANS

My interest is in the future because I am going to spend the rest of my life there.
—Charles F. Kettering, American engineer

Let's face it. Some of us who choose careers in music tend not to be particularly interested in business or personal finance. This is no surprise since music and business seem to fall at opposite ends of the left-brain–right-brain spectrum.

In some cases, freelance musicians can have unpredictable, lower-than-average income, or a lack of employer-sponsored health and life insurance and retirement benefits. These factors make it especially important that musicians manage their finances wisely. Even if you are fortunate enough to have a job that offers excellent benefits, it is worth noting that government and private retirement programs are not immune to the effects of financial crises, so it is important to be proactive in creating your own pathway to financial security.

Saving for Your Future

The first step toward improving your financial security is to adopt the mindset that you are going to save for the future and limit debt as much as possible. If you must incur debt, formulate a plan to pay it back as quickly as possible and make this your first priority. To do this, you need to live within your means, minimize your spending, and be creative about ways to increase your income as a young musician. Some potential ways to increase your income include teaching private or group lessons, working for a music store, working at band camps, playing and doing instrument demonstrations for school assembly programs, seeking playing engagements such as weddings and other church services, providing background music at events with chamber groups, and eventually, solo and ensemble performances.

Recordkeeping

The next step is to get an accurate picture of your current situation and keep track of how you spend your money. Computer programs such as Intuit's *Quicken* are easy to use and can download data directly from your financial institution. Once you learn to enter transaction details accurately, these programs can quickly and easily provide reports summarizing your financial activities.

Smartphone users can download a free application called *Mint.com*. It allows users to see all their accounts in one place, set budgets, and find personalized savings options by comparing products such as credit cards, certificates of deposit, and online bill paying services.

Detailed information about personal financial management is available from many sources, including www.inc.com/guides/create-personal-financial-statement .html, SuzeOrman.com, and the books listed in this tip.

Ignoring your finances is not an option. Whether you do your own bookkeeping or seek assistance from a qualified expert, recordkeeping is not only critical to your financial success, but the IRS requires that you keep track of your income and expenses for income tax purposes. Be sure to consult a tax professional for proper handling of these items.

Basic Principles

It is important to manage your finances properly to make progress. Some basic suggestions are:

- Don't spend money you don't have.
- Build up a "rainy day" fund in an amount equivalent to six months of living expenses (housing, food, insurance, bills). You will sleep better knowing you sacrificed material things and gained some financial security.
- Pay your bills on time. Failure to meet your obligations can have a negative impact on your credit rating and on your ability to do business in the future.
- Do not sign up for credit cards without reading the fine print or knowing how they work.
- Credit cards should be paid in full each month. Carrying balances is a sign that one is spending beyond their means.
- According to financial experts, it is critical to start saving as early as possible. The concept of compound interest is powerful and the sooner you begin to save, the better. For example, $5,000 invested and earning a 5 percent annual return will grow to approximately $8,000 in 10 years, $13,000 in 20 years, and to over $21,000 in 30 years.

Managing Your Investments

Once you have some savings, you need to decide how to manage your balance. It may be safest to keep your money in an insured bank account, but this also guarantees that your money will generate only limited returns. In general, taking greater risks can result in greater gains. The longer you have until retirement, the more risk you can afford to take. Consult with a well-respected investment advisor or firm to determine a path that will help you reach your long-term goals.

Take a College Course

Many colleges offer personal finance courses, providing a structured setting in which to learn about sound money management practices that can significantly impact your future financial situation.

Suggested Reading

The excellent book *The Savvy Musician*, by David Cutler, includes twenty-two pages on personal finance. The author reminds musicians that they devote countless hours in the practice room and that taking a few hours out of their practice schedule to read about personal finance could dramatically impact their future financial success. He also cleverly compares music with finances, as both take education, practice, patience, discipline, and a clear plan.

Personal finance is discussed in detail in a book entitled *Financial Management for Musicians*, by Pam Gaines and Cathy McCormack. While this book was published over ten years ago and is generally aimed at popular musicians, the basic principles still hold true. It includes a CD with Excel and Lotus spreadsheet files such as tax reports, personal budget, equipment list, sales log for recordings, mileage log, revenue log, personal net worth, business use of home, and business expenses.

More recent books aimed at the general public are listed below, including titles that focus on helping and guiding young people who might have accrued debt and face a weak job market. Good books on personal finance usually are not about accumulating great wealth quickly, but instead give you sound advice about how to gradually achieve financial security. Here are some suggested reading materials:

- *The Complete Idiot's Guide to Personal Finance in Your 20s and 30s*, by Sarah Young Fisher and Susan Shelly.
- *Personal Finance for Dummies*, by Eric Tyson.
- *The Everything Book: Personal Finance in Your 20s and 30s: Erase Your Debt, Personalize Your Budget, and Plan Now to Secure Your Future*, by Debby Fowles.
- *1,001 Things They Won't Tell You: An Insider's Guide to Spending, Saving, and Living Wisely*, by Jonathan Dahl.
- *Pay It Down! From Debt to Wealth on $10 a Day*, by Jean Chatzky.
- *The Money Book for the Young, Fabulous and Broke*, by Suze Orman.
- Along with the many books she published, Suze Orman offers a wealth of free and priceless resources to her readers, such as her educational videos on YouTube and podcasts on iTunes, as well as her website SuzeOrman .com that includes web tools like Debt Eliminator and Expense Tracker. She

hosts a television show, a radio show, web events, and tours the world as a motivational speaker.

It has been said that *good things come to those who wait.* It takes patience to let your money grow over long periods of time. It is also true that *the early bird gets the worm.* The sooner one starts saving, the sooner the benefits will be realized, so be proactive with your personal finances and start a savings plan.

QUICK TIP 93: CREATING AND POSTING YOUR PROFESSIONAL WEBSITE

Creating and posting your own website is essential for building a personal and professional network in the music world. Will Cicola, my former graduate student, and currently a doctoral candidate at Michigan State University, offers the following advice.

An online website builder tool is the quickest and easiest way to build a website. There are many options such as iWeb, designed specifically for Mac at apple.com/ilife/iweb, and PageBreeze for Windows. Others include pagebreeze.com, freewebs.com, and webstarts.com, which are free and easy to use. They allow you to create your website in the same way you would design a brochure or concert program with a choice of templates to help you with the initial creative process. You can also use Google's free sites tool at sites.google.com, which lets you create a website from within any browser and even assigns you a URL.

Posting Your Website

If you are using Google Pages, Google will store your website on their servers for free. Otherwise, you will need a hosting service in order to make your website accessible to the outside world. Companies such as GoDaddy.com, Justhost.com, and Bluehost.com offer inexpensive hosting and domain name registration that lets others access your website by typing www.yournamehere.com. Additionally, they provide technical support to help you get your website online.

Promoting Your Website

To be effective, your website must be easily accessible. Ideally, you want it to be one of the first results that appear when your name is searched. Some companies specialize in helping website owners increase their ranking in Google. Not everyone needs to take such extreme measures, but there are a few quick and easy things you can do to boost your ranking in search engine results.

The first step is to register your site using Google's Webmaster Tools at google.com/webmasters. In addition to telling Google that your site exists, this allows you to see how people are discovering and reaching your page.

Once you are listed on Google, the best way to rise in their rankings is by linking. Add links to the websites of your school, organization, your teachers and colleagues, and request that they link to you. Google tends to list social networking sites first (such as Facebook, LinkedIn, and Twitter) so update your profiles on those sites with links to your website.

Another way to increase your visibility is to add your URL to a service such as Submit Express at submitexpress.com that allows you to enter keywords and choose which search engines will include your website.

Testing Your Website

To make sure most users can view your site, test it with major browsers such as Internet Explorer, and the latest versions of Firefox, Opera, and Safari. These browsers are free and easy to install.

QUICK TIP 94: DESIGNING YOUR PROFESSIONAL WEBSITE

Once you have settled your domain name and web host, the next step is to design the website itself. Nearly everyone uses the Internet to do business and to search for information, so it is essential to create a professional-looking website. Your website should emphasize specific categories depending upon whether you are primarily a performing musician or an educator.

All websites begin with a homepage. You get only a few seconds to make a good impression, so this page should be striking. Its content should be limited to the basics, such as your name, photo, contact information, your professional focus, and some current information. The goal is to provide enough information to allow viewers to quickly decide if they are interested in learning more about you. If the homepage is too detailed and cluttered, web surfers are likely to be overwhelmed and simply jump to another site. You may want to take the time to visit a professional photographer who will take high-quality shots of you for your site.

The links on your homepage should include a biography page with your education and main performance and work experience. Be sure that the information is well organized, accurate, and free of typos and errors. Anything less will present a negative image of you and your work.

Media content is a very important component of a musician's website. Create a media page that includes audio and video files representing your best performances. Note that a good performance that is poorly recorded will not reflect your best work, so include only top-quality files. If you are an active performer, list your upcoming events and concerts, press reviews, and examples of recital or masterclass programs you offer.

Music educators should include their philosophy of teaching, describe their students' achievements or activities, private lesson details, and a list of publications. Musicians should not expect to be accomplished web designers overnight; however, the many website building programs available today simplify the process significantly. It is always a good idea to seek assistance from experienced webmasters to ensure success. Before you enlist their help, make sure you have a clear idea on how you wish your website to look like. The best way to convey your ideas and vision is to provide your web specialist with a navigation map listing individual page titles, content, graphics, layout, and how the links will be organized.

If free online website builder tools and webmasters fall short, you can opt to pay a fee and use web building sites such as intuit.com or homestead.com.

QUICK TIP 95: CLARINET PARENT'S GUIDE

When I invite prospective students to visit my clarinet studio at Miami University, I ask parents to join in to observe a lesson and chat afterward. One of the first things I look for in future students is parental support. Without this important element, the numerous challenges faced by college music students can become overwhelming.

My friend Chris Jones is the webmaster of Clarinet-Now.com. He offers parents the following *Steps to Improve Your Young Clarinetist's Musical Experience:*

1. Provide a quiet and comfortable practice space with good lighting, preferably away from siblings, TV, computer, video games, iPod, cell phone, and other potential distractions.
2. A good-quality instrument and mouthpiece will help young players excel. It is not necessary to provide the most expensive equipment for beginners, but very inexpensive gear is likely to be an impediment to the student's development. Also consider good used instruments instead of inexpensive new ones.
3. Be sure to keep a steady supply of new reeds, as well as accessories such as cork grease, cleaning swab, small screwdriver, mirror, music stand, metronome, and tuner.
4. Keep your child's clarinet in good working order with regular maintenance performed by a qualified repair technician.
5. Encourage your young clarinetist to listen to professional recordings and live concerts. Exposure to high-level performances should include clarinetists and a wide variety of other instruments and vocalists.
6. Support participation in as many musical activities as possible. These events may include honor bands, all-county bands, solo and ensemble contests, and recitals.
7. If your child shows keen interest in the clarinet, you may want to seek recommendations to locate a private clarinet teacher for regular applied lessons.
8. Find opportunities for your child to interact with musicians who have comparable and more advanced skills. Playing duets with clarinetists, flutists, saxophonists, or any other combination is a great way to stimulate their interest in playing.
9. Encourage your child to perform for family and friends. The experience will be excellent preparation for performances in other settings.
10. Support your child by attending their music events and by joining musical organizations for parents.
11. Find ways to encourage your young clarinetist to be self-motivated to practice regularly. Success is more likely for students who enjoy playing than for those who are pressured into doing so.
12. Purchase fun educational tools such as play-along CDs and a SmartMusic interactive accompaniment online subscription available at smartmusic.com.

Parental support can mean the difference between a special talent flourishing or disappearing. If music is to be an important part of your life, share your insight with your parents and ask them for their support and involvement. You may also recommend helpful books on the topic such as Michelle Siteman's *The Pleasures and Perils of Raising Young Musicians: A Guide for Parents*, and Elaine Schmidt's *Hey Mom! Listen to This! A Parent's Guide to Music*, and Amy Nathan's *The Young Musician's Guide Survival Guide: Tips from Teens and Pros*.

Another very helpful book is *Tipbook Clarinet: The Complete Guide*, by Hugo Piksterboer, published by Hal Leonard. Aimed at beginner and intermediate clarinetists, it contains a wealth of information about the clarinet's history, as well as tips regarding lessons, practicing, auditions, selection of instruments and accessories, maintenance, tuning, and reed fixing. The book also includes a resource guide and a fingering chart. The design of this book is attractive, impeccable, and very innovative in that it directs readers to a series of short online videos. Visit tipbook.com.

QUICK TIP 96: PREPARING YOUR MUSIC BEFORE THE PERFORMANCE

Your sheet music will never fall off your stand except on the very hour of your concert. —Murphy's Law

Although it might seem like a small detail at first, one should not underestimate the importance of preparing sheet music before a performance. Dropping a loose sheet of music in the middle of an exposed part is a sure way to make it fall flat, literally. Here are simple ways to prepare music parts:

1. If more than two pages need to be placed together on a stand, secure pages together from top to bottom with clear adhesive tape so they will remain in the proper order. This also helps the music to stay flat on the stand.
2. Carefully plan your music so that page turns are efficient and practical. This might mean rearranging certain pages or cutting them horizontally in two (the binding will hold the separated sections together) so that the top part can be turned first and the bottom part later during a rest.
3. If the music consists of a collection of loose sheets, clearly number each one so that the order is correct each time.
4. If you change the order of movements for any reason, clearly note this in your music so that you won't forget during the performance. Stage anxiety can result in surprising memory slips, so it is better to be safe than sorry.
5. Clearly mark your music with special dynamics or tempo changes. This saves time during practice and also helps you to recall the smallest details during performances. You may choose to write in pencil or a color pen or highlighter for crucial information; however, this should of course not be done on rental parts or borrowed parts, and pencil markings should be erased before returning rentals. Naturally, borrowed parts should not be marked in any way.
6. If you wish to play a piece without turning pages, consider reducing its size by cutting all margins and attaching the pages together so that they will all fit together on the stand. If reduction is not practical, plan to use two stands and practice with both stands beforehand. Note that photocopying published music is illegal.
7. Don't wait until the last minute to plan your sheet music setup, as tricky page turns need to be practiced ahead of time.
8. If a page needs to be unfolded from the part before the performance, mark "unfold page" at the very top of your first page.
9. When marking your chamber music parts, refrain from writing colleagues' names as cues ("Mike" or "Angie"), as chamber music personnel changes

on a regular basis. Instead, write the instrument's cue, such as "horn cue" or "oboe cue." Planning ahead can make the difference between a successful performance and a disappointing one. As the Girl Scouts and Boy Scouts say: *Be prepared!*

QUICK TIP 97: RECORDING YOUR PRACTICE SESSIONS

Recording your practice sessions gives you the opportunity to act as your own teacher. Hiring yourself as your own teacher is not only a clever timesaver, it is a sure bet, and free of charge. Students often avoid recording their practice sessions because they dislike hearing themselves. However, what they hear is what the teacher will hear in the lesson. Wouldn't it make more sense to record passages repeatedly and make adjustments until the student is happy with the result, ultimately increasing the likelihood that the teacher will concur?

When practicing, it is a challenge to objectively assess progress for several reasons:

1. The way you hear yourself in your head is very different from how you really sound, so recording your practice sessions allows you to hear yourself as others hear you.
2. While practicing, you may overlook some details because you are busy concentrating on technical problems or playing the correct notes. Even when playing passages over and over, chances are that some details will be neglected, which can eventually affect the outcome of an audition or a performance. Naturally, it does take a little bravery to record your playing, and even more nerve to listen to the result. Also, it takes patience because recording yourself requires you to pause between passages in order to operate the electronic equipment. If you are pressed for time, you might prefer to simply skip the recording process, but ultimately we play to be heard so it is important to practice in a setting that emulates a live performance. The audio recorder is a great tool to reveal small details that can get past us while practicing, such as intonation subtleties or tempo variations.
3. Instrumentalists can be so busy playing that they are "hearing" but not really *listening*. Recording yourself makes you more aware of your playing, which makes you a much better listener and critical thinker. In time, you will be able to evaluate your playing more efficiently and accelerate your progress.

A full circle is established when we:

1. Play
2. Assess our playing
3. Take corrective action
4. Repeat the passage with more awareness

Three effective methods of recording yourself include an audio digital recorder, computer software such as *Audacity* or *GarageBand* (both available online free of charge), and SmartMusic, which can be downloaded by purchasing a very afford-able yearly subscription at smartmusic.com.

High-quality portable digital audio recorders are readily available and afford-able. Electronic equipment can become obsolete in a matter of just a few months; however, popular examples at the moment are the Zoom H2 Handy Portable Stereo Recorder and the Edirol R-09HR High-Resolution WAVE/MP3 Recorder. Here are some tips for recording your practice sessions:

1. Listen and evaluate your playing by noting observations in your music with a pencil.
2. Hear notes before your fingers play them and pay attention to details in tone, articulation, rhythm, intonation, phrasing, and air speed variation. Always "dress up" your tone as if you were playing in a concert hall.
3. Use a metronome to assess your progress with technique and tonguing tem-pos. Keeping track of maximum tempos achieved while maintaining clean playing results in progress that can be measured.
4. Listen to high-quality professional recordings of the piece you are practicing and try to emulate the overall result.
5. Record yourself in various situations such as solo playing, duo with piano accompaniment, and with large ensembles. Remember to ask for permission before recording other musicians.
6. Record as you practice with a play-along CD.
7. After listening to your recording a few times during your practice session, wait a couple of days to clear your mind and listen to it once again with a fresh set of ears.
8. Collect your recorded clips and file them on your computer. Create separate folders for each piece and organize them in chronological order. You can then listen to your progress and assess variants such as speed, tone, and phrasing improvement. Over time, your sound clip collection will be sizable and will clearly demonstrate your progress.
9. After a year or so, choose one audio clip from your modest beginnings and another after months of hard work. Have your fellow classmates listen to and compare your "before and after" sound files. The progress demonstrated will undoubtedly convince interested parties to emulate your journey.

QUICK TIP 98: KEEP A PRACTICE JOURNAL

A journal is a very efficient way to keep track of one's progress in the practice room. It can be surprising how quickly important details can be forgotten, and how making note of daily improvements can be a great motivator in order to reach goals. Journals can be useful for all kinds of other endeavors as well. For example, some body builders maintain their motivation by keeping track of their exercise routine in a journal and by creating video blogs of their gradual physical transformations.

Here are some suggestions on how to keep a journal to maximize the effectiveness of your daily practice:

1. If you are taking lessons, find a quiet spot immediately after each session to write down the ideas you found most helpful. This way, you will remember the new concepts to work on without interrupting the lesson to take notes.
2. If you have a particular problem (with tonguing, for example), write down various corrective methods you used and after a few days, make note of those that work best. This will also help you design your pedagogy later on if you enter the teaching profession.
3. Find ways to measure your progress quantitatively. For example, write down the metronome tempos attained for certain exercises and use this information as a basis of comparison for future results. You can keep track of your tonguing and technical progress, the timing of your long tones (measured in seconds), and so on.
4. Draw graphics to illustrate certain points. For example, draw the embouchure concepts you learned to clarify your own perception, and as mentioned previously, to help develop your pedagogical skills as a future teacher.
5. Write down how you practice and keep a schedule to make sure you use your time as efficiently as possible. For example, list elements included in your practice. These items could include:

- Warm up body (arms, hands, wrists, neck, and shoulders).
- Ten minutes of long tones.
- Ten minutes of scales.
- Fifteen minutes of etudes.
- Five-minute break (to avoid tendon injuries).
- Thirty minutes of solo repertoire.
- Fifteen minutes of orchestral, band, or chamber music excerpts.
- Warm down body for a few minutes.

The preceding items amount to about one and one-half hours of practice material. Naturally, the list will vary depending on individual situations and you may want to request assistance from your teacher to design an appropriate practice schedule.

6. List items to be learned or improved upon in the future and check off each item as you achieve it. This helps monitor your progress and gives you a sense of accomplishment as you go down the list, not to mention that it will prevent you from overlooking important points. Some items might include increasing tempos of specific technical passages each day, or the number of bars you were able to memorize, or how fast you could tongue a staccato passage. Also, write down the specific repertoire you practiced during your session and keep track of how much you mastered within each piece or excerpt. Writing down your observations about your practice also makes you a sharper observer because it will make you more aware of details to work on once you know in advance that you plan on taking notes on a weekly basis.
7. Write questions to ask your teacher during your next lesson. Mark your music and refer to related questions in your journal. It is easy to forget important questions while concentrating on your lesson, so bring your journal to your lesson, and ask away.

These are only a few suggestions. You will undoubtedly come up with your own ideas as you progress. The main objective is to make sure you dedicate a special notebook for this and not dilute it with other subjects. If preferred, a binder can be used so that pages can be removed or moved around if needed.

Later on, you will appreciate having saved the information, especially if you become a professional performer or teacher.

Ready-made Practice Journals

Ready-made music practice notebooks help improve practice habits and can be used as practice journals as well. They are excellent motivational tools that can provide incentive when inspiration is running low. Examples are the *Music Practice Book* (Music Sales Corporation), which features a double-page spread to note your goals, assignments, and progress, as well as staves for music notation. Another example is *Practice Planner: A Journal of Goals and Progress* by reed instrument specialist Harvey R. Snitkin. It includes tips on how to set goals in manageable increments, thirty-six lesson assignment charts designed to last a school year, as well as motivational text related to practice, technique, and musicianship. *The Art of Practicing: A Guide to Making Music from the Heart* by Madeline Bruser, is a spiral-bound notebook created to help keep track of many specific areas of performance practice on a daily basis. The spiral binding helps to keep the book flat when you write new entries at various times during your practice. Finally, Burton Kaplan's *Musician's Practice Log* helps players plan their practice a day and/or a week ahead. It includes erasable, laminated sheets with areas to write goals and stay motivated.

Books

A great way to reflect on practicing is to read books on the subject. Several authors offer helpful and detailed pointers to improve practice routines. Books aimed at young instrumentalists include Amy Nathan's *The Young Musician's Survival Guide: Tips from Teens and Pros*, and Harvey Snitkin's *Practicing for Young Musicians: You Are Your Own Teacher*. Both writers focus on techniques to help aspiring musicians develop a healthy attitude toward practicing, how to manage practice time, and how to combat performance anxiety.

For advanced instrumentalists, I recommend Stewart Gordon's *Mastering the Art of Performance: A Primer for Musicians*, which is an in-depth guide for musicians aspiring to reach the highest level of performance. The author provides detailed advice on various practice and self-evaluation techniques, warm-up exercises, goal setting, and stage fright. Another book is *The Practice Revolution: Getting Great Results from the Six Days between Lessons* by Philip Johnston. Johnston argues that the actual lesson hour is only a small fraction of a student's entire musical training experience, and that students must use the time between lessons as efficiently as possible. He offers solutions to various problematic practice techniques that might be holding a student back, as well as advice regarding time management issues. The book includes tips on memorization as well as various musical games to alleviate performance anxiety.

Paperless Practice

Technology enthusiasts might prefer to use a computer or handheld device instead of paper to record their progress and practice goals. Whichever format you choose, make sure your notes are easily accessible for quick reference and note taking. You may also try trading journal notes with a peer to compare experiences and exchange practice strategies, and you may even wish to blog some of your entries.

Room to Grow

It is important to remember that for good practice, one needs to set up a practice space that will be conducive to productive work. Necessities include a comfortable chair, a good music stand, good lighting, a clean surface for reeds, a sound system or computer to play-along recordings or work with the SmartMusic system, and all necessary accessories such as a metronome, tuner, recording device, mirror, clarinet stand, pencil, and your notebook.

QUICK TIP 99: QUICK-ADVICE BULLETIN BOARD—EXTRA TIPS

- Learn to sing. Singing is a great way to conceptualize wind control more clearly and improve listening skills.
- When practicing technical passages, learn to see the big picture as well as details. Instead of focusing solely on technical challenges within a musical phrase, take a "step back to see the forest for the trees" and envision the overall phrase's line and direction.
- Embrace technology. Musicians need to remember that technology impacts their work significantly on a daily basis. Musicians now self-produce professional-quality recordings, create promotional websites, and advertise and teach online. Having the vision to use technology to help further your career is essential.
- Listen to recordings of master musicians. Listening to great performers is a lesson in itself, especially when you listen to your favorite recordings over and over. The more times you listen, the more details become apparent, which in turn can be imitated more easily. Also, great, live performances can be viewed on YouTube.com. YouTube allows us to virtually jump into a time machine and experience vintage performances that were never previously available. Additionally, YouTube gives us access to recitals by musicians from distant lands who may not yet be well known internationally or have recorded CDs. Lastly, YouTube allows us to view an array of live performances that could previously be seen only by a select few.
- Join the International Clarinet Association (ICA), which offers a quarterly subscription to a stellar clarinet magazine called *The Clarinet*. The ICA is an organization that meets in various locations within the United States and around the world for their annual event called ClarinetFest. It supports an extensive research library with materials available to all members, and promotes a variety of endeavors related to clarinet such as performance competitions, research, and composition projects. To join the ICA, visit clarinet.org.
- Join the Clarinet and Saxophone Society of Great Britain. Like the ICA, they offer a beautiful quarterly magazine titled *Clarinet and Saxophone*. Visit cassgb.org.
- Join the Australian Clarinet and Saxophone Association. They also publish a magazine called *Australian Clarinet and Saxophone*. Visit clarinet-saxophone.asn.au.

- Visit Chris Jones' extensive clarinet website called clarinet-now.com. Jones exposes students to just about everything under the sun such as: tips on practicing, technique, sight-reading, various articles, blogs, MP3s, videos, reeds, equipment, vendors, theory, and information about notable artists.
- Read books on your instrument. The largest collection of clarinet books offered for purchase online is available at Van Cott Information Services, Inc. Visit vcisinc.com.
- For a list of thirty-two more quick tips as well as a career planning exercise, see Secret 52: Last-Minute Secrets in my first book, *Clarinet Secrets*.

QUICK TIP 100: MY OWN QUICK TIPS

The best way to learn is to teach, and the best way to teach is to keep learning. You can use this page to create your own list of Quick Tips and share it with others.

1. _____
_____

2. _____
_____

3. _____
_____

4. _____
_____

5. _____
_____

6. _____
_____

7. _____
_____

8. _____
_____

9. _____
_____

10. _____
_____

Index

accompaniment, 25, 37, 38, 97, 104, 105,
    106, 136, 145; interactive, 42, 136, 171;
    piano, 42, 105, 108, 145, 160, 176
air: leaking, 15, 79; management, 13, 20;
    speed, 18, 176
airflow, 13, 19, 20, 23, 25, 28, 31, 41, 85,
    89, 129
altissimo register, 2, 3
articulation, 36, 37, 41, 44, 80, 88, 89, 90,
    158, 176
audio recorders, 176
auditions, 33, 172; bass clarinet, 86;
    college, 159, 160; E♭ orchestral, 84;
    military band, 94, 96; orchestral, 86,
    87, 157
Australian Clarinet and Saxophone
    Association, 181

baroque, 91, 92, 98, 118, 119
bass clarinet: etudes, 88; method books, 88
basset horn, 86, 88, 115
biting, 3, 13, 18, 19, 22, 23, 26, 28, 55, 61,
    72, 76, 85
blood oxygenation, 31
books, 88, 104, 105, 106, 107, 119, 120,
    179; bass clarinet, 88; business, 151,
    152; excerpt, 81, 82, 84; fitness and
    wellness, 124, 125; health, 123, 142;
    interviewing, 164; jazz, 90; klezmer,
    110; marketability, 163; performance

anxiety, 139; personal finance, 166,
    167; practicing, 179; self-help, 172;
    self-improvement, 141, 151
bore: oil, 49, 50
braces, 56
breath marks, 31
breathing, 31, 40, 88, 125, 131, 133;
    exercises, 121, 122, 141

clarinet, 84; A, 84, 98, 115; alto, 88, 110,
    114; bass, 53, 86, 87, 88, 91, 111, 112,
    113, 115; basset, 86, 88; C, 84, 86, 98,
    115; contrabass, 86, 88; D, 84, 86, 87;
    E♭, 53, 81, 84, 85, 86, 87, 91, 111, 116;
    G, 101; maintenance, 60, 171, 172;
    repair, 49, 51, 53, 54, 60, 74, 78, 171;
    second, 81, 82, 87
Clarinet and Saxophone Society of Great
    Britain, 181
Claripatch, 52
concert(s), 53, 102, 123, 124, 129, 137,
    141, 143, 145, 147; attendance, 149,
    171; dress code, 143; tours, 94; venue,
    134
conference: clarinet, 46
cork, 60, 75, 78; grease, 60, 75, 79, 171;
    joint, 78; key, 57, 58, 78; natural, 78;
    tenon joint, 75, 78, 79
cracking, 49, 51, 60
creativity, 34, 103, 152, 155, 156

About the Author

Michele Gingras is professor of music at Miami University in Oxford, Ohio, where she was named Crossan Hays Curry Distinguished Educator and Distinguished Scholar of the Graduate Faculty. She performed worldwide, including at sixteen International Clarinet Association conferences, recorded over a dozen CDs, and also performs as a klezmer musician and with her chamber groups Duo2go and Miami3. She published one book, *Clarinet Secrets: 52 Performance Strategies for the Advanced Clarinetist* (Scarecrow Press, 2004/Revised 2006), and over 160 articles, columns, and reviews for international publications. She earned a *Premier Prix* at the Montreal Conservatory, a M.M. at Northwestern University, and did doctoral work at Indiana University. She is past-secretary of the International Clarinet Association and an artist clinician for Rico International and Buffet Crampon USA. Subscribe to her free clarinet video podcasts on iTunes and visit her website at michelegingras.com.

Printed in Great Britain
by Amazon.co.uk, Ltd.,
Marston Gate.